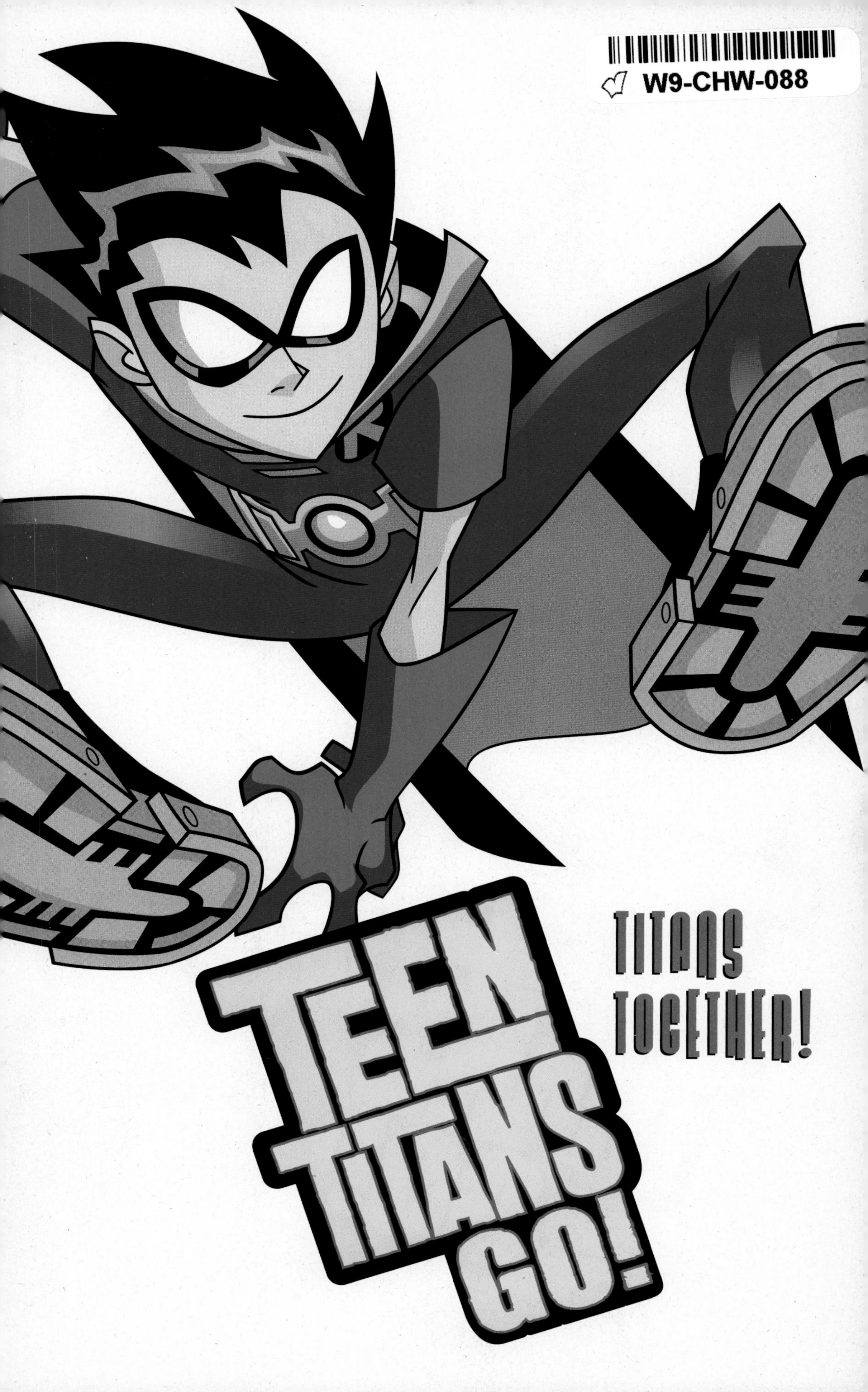

W9-CHW-088
TEEN TITANS GO!
TITANS TOGETHER!

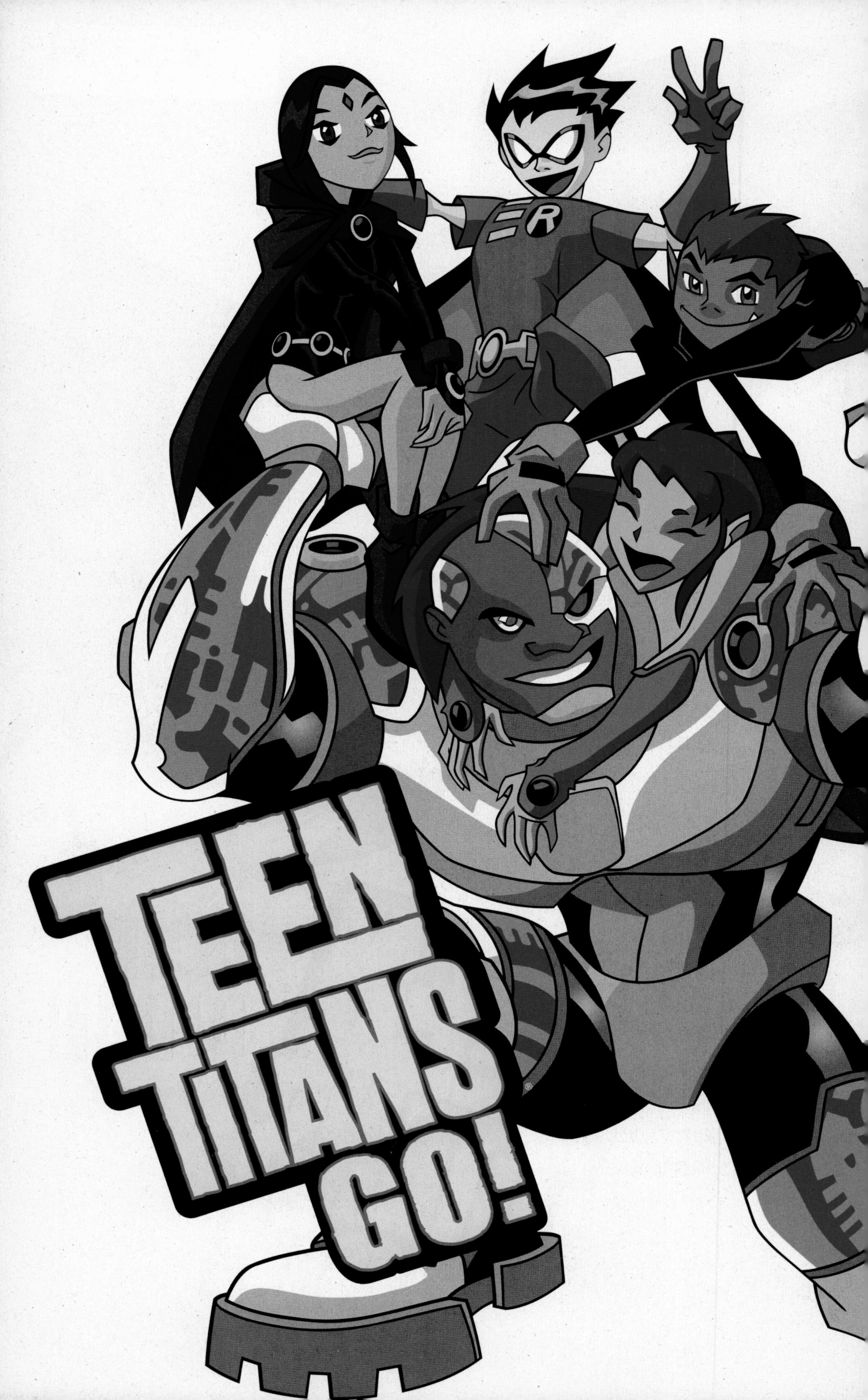
TEEN TITANS GO!

TITANS TOGETHER!

J. TORRES WRITER

COLORS BY HEROIC AGE

(UNLESS OTHERWISE NOTED)

Cover illustration by Todd Nauck Cover color by Kanilla Tripp

TEEN TITANS GO! TITANS TOGETHER!

This label only applies to the text section.

DC Comics, 4000 Warner Blvd., Burbank, CA 91522
A Warner Bros. Entertainment Company.
Printed by Transcontinental Interglobe, Beauceville, QC, Canada. 4/10/15. Second Printing.
ISBN: 978-1-4012-5367-7

Library of Congress Cataloging-in-Publication Data
J. Torres.
Teen titans go!. Titans together / J. Torres, Mike Norton.
pages cm
Summary: "The all-ages collection featuring TEEN TITANS GO! #27-32 is back in print, with the team's battles with Jinx, Mas y Menos, Dr. Light and more! Plus, appearances by the Doom Patrol and Nightwing!"– Provided by publisher.
ISBN 978-1-4012-5367-7
1. Graphic novels. I. Norton, Mike. II. Title. III. Title: Titans Together.
PZ7.7 .T42 2014
741.5'973–dc23
2012474779

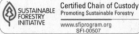

TINSELTOWN
THAT'S IT, BIRD BRAIN! FOLLOW GIZMO!
!
CRASH!
"O" MY! THAT HAD TO HURT! HAW-HAW!

DID YOU SEE THAT!

HE'S *PERFECT!*

LOOK OUT!

TEEN TITANS PASSING THROUGH!

OKAY...THAT **HURT...**

WHERE'D GIZMO GO...?

WE'LL CATCH UP TO HIM **LATER!** ARE YOU **ALL RIGHT?**

LET ME GIVE YOU A HAND.

OOOH, THAT FEELS NICE...LIKE A WARM SOY BATH...

CALL OF THE WILD
CAN YOU BELIEVE IT! ME! A MOVIE STAR!
SUPA STAR

DON'T YOU HAVE TO ACTUALLY STAR IN A MOVIE BEFORE YOU CAN CALL YOURSELF A MOVIE STAR?

UH, ***HELLO?*** TINSELTOWN STUDIOS' "JUNGLE BOY" STARRING BEAST BOY COMING SOON TO A THEATER NEAR YOU!

SO, YOU'VE DECIDED THEN...

YOU'RE DOING THE MOVIE FOR ***SURE?***

COME ON, I'VE ALWAYS WONDERED WHAT IT WOULD BE LIKE TO BE IN THE MOVIES...I'VE GOT THE ***LOOKS,*** THE ***CHARISMA...***

AND LIKE THOSE STUDIO PEOPLE SAID, I'VE GOT ***"STAR QUALITY,"*** RIGHT?

GEE, THANKS FOR THE SUPPORT, GUYS! I'LL TRY TO REMEMBER YOU IN ALL OF MY AWARD ACCEPTANCE SPEECHES...
BUT BEAST BOY, DO YOU EVEN KNOW HOW TO ACT?
WELL, HE IS THE BIGGEST DRAMA QUEEN I KNOW.

TINSELTOWN
TINSELTOWN STUDIOS
SORRY...
...I DON'T SEE ANY "ROBO BOY" ON THE LIST.
THE NAME'S CYBORG, FUNNY GUY.
AND THIS HERE'S BEAST BOY, STAR OF "JUNGLE BOY."
BEAST BOY! WHY DIDN'T YOU SAY SO?!
SO SORRY, SIR! I DIDN'T REALIZE IT WAS YOU!
GEE, MAYBE THE GREEN SKIN AND HAIR SHOULD'VE GIVEN HIM AWAY?

YOU CAN
RIGHT IN, SIR...
...THEY'RE WAITING FOR YOU ON SOUND STAGE 7...
TUESDAYS WITH STUCKER
...HOPE YOU LIKE YOUR DRESSING ROOM--I HELPED PICK OUT THE WALLPAPER!
PALMINATOR 2
DEADLINE
EXPLODY! THE MOVIE!
BUT YOU'RE STILL NOT ON THE LIST! SO, YOU NEED TO GET THIS CAR OUT OF THE DRIVEWAY AND STOP BLOCKING THE GATE!
WHAT?! BUT WE'RE WITH HIM!
TH-THIS SET IS C-CLOSED TO ENTOURAGES, POSSES, AND OTHER L-LEECHES!
LEECHES?! WHO YOU CALLIN' A LEECH?! WE'RE HIS TEAMMATES! WE'RE HERE TO "SUPPORT" HIM!
FORGET IT, CYBORG! WE CAN CHECK IN ON BEAST BOY LATER, BUT RIGHT NOW...
...WE'VE GOT TROUBLE!

-DUUUDE, I COULD SO GET USED TO THIS!
SO, IS EVERYTHING TO YOUR LIKING, SIR?
WELL, EVERYTHING EXCEPT...THAT.
YOU DON'T LIKE THE SWAN SCULPTURE OF PATÉ MADE BY CELEBRITY CHEF PIERRE OF THE EXCLUSIVE BISTRO FOOFOO?
BUT ALL THE YOUNG HOT MOVIE ACTORS REQUEST ONE FOR THEIR DRESSING ROOMS THESE DAYS!
UM, I'M A VEGETARIAN. I DON'T EAT MEAT.
-GASP!-
--I AM SO, SO, SO SORRY, SIR!
CODE RED! CODE RED! CHOP-CHOP, PEOPLE! MEAT EXTRACTION! CODE RED!

TODD & LARY GO TO FRIGHT CASTLE
THE LIVER SPREAD SCULPTURE HAS BEEN TAKEN CARE OF. ANYTHING ELSE, SIR?
UM...I DON'T LIKE EVERYONE CALLING ME "SIR." HOW ABOUT...
...MR. BEAST BOY INSTEAD!
BEAST BOY, BABY! TOMMIE P.! THAT'S TOMMIE WITH AN "I-E" AND P WITH A PERIOD.
I'M THE FIRST ASSISTANT DIRECTOR TO THE SECOND ASSISTANT DIRECTOR OF THE THIRD UNIT!
FIRST ASSISTANT WHAT TO THE DIRECTOR OF THE WHAT...?
EXPLODEY II
DON'T WORRY ABOUT IT, BABE. IT JUST MEANS THAT I'LL BE DIRECTING YOU IN ALL OF YOUR SCENES.
HAVE YOU READ THE LATEST DRAFT OF THE SCRIPT?
YES, AND I ACTUALLY HAVE SOME QUESTIONS...
GOOD, GOOD, QUESTIONS ARE GOOD...
BUT MAKE SURE YOU LOOK OVER THIS MORNING'S REWRITES AND ALL OF THE DIRECTOR'S NOTES...
...AND DON'T HESITATE TO LET FOOD SERVICES KNOW IF YOU NEED ANY MORE JELLYBEANS OR MINERAL WATER OR WHATEVER...
...I'LL SEE YOU ON THE SET IN FIVE MINUTES!
SCRIPT
JUNGLE BOY

DROP IT, JINX. IT DOESN'T HAVE TO BE THIS WAY...
BANK
NO...
...YOU DROP! AND GIVE ME TWENTY, SOLDIER!
KLANG
DON'T KNOW ABOUT TWENTY, PRIVATE HIVE, BUT HOW ABOUT...
...FIVE!
OR HOW ABOUT FIFTEEN?
AS IN SIZE FIF--
ONE SECOND, PLEASE, I SHOULD TAKE THIS CALL...

B.B.! BEEN WAITING TO HEAR FROM YOU, DUDE! I THOUGHT YOU FORGOT ALL ABOUT US LITTLE PEOPLE!
I HATE CELL PHONES!
IT'S CALLED A T-COMMUNICATOR!
OOF!
HOW GOES IT, SUPERSTAR? MEET ANY CUTE, AVAILABLE ACTRESSES? GOT ANY PHONE NUMBERS FOR ME?
CUTE ACTRESSES?
REALLY? THAT MUCH FOOD? AND IT'S FREE! JELLYBEANS, TOO! WHOA, TALK ABOUT STAR TREATMENT! NO WONDER WE HAVEN'T HEARD FROM YOU IN DAYS!
CYBORG! THEY'RE GETTING AWAY!
UH, LISTEN, I SHOULD LET YOU GO...
I'M SURE YOU'VE GOT LINES TO RUN OR WHATEVER YOU MOVIE PEOPLE DO...

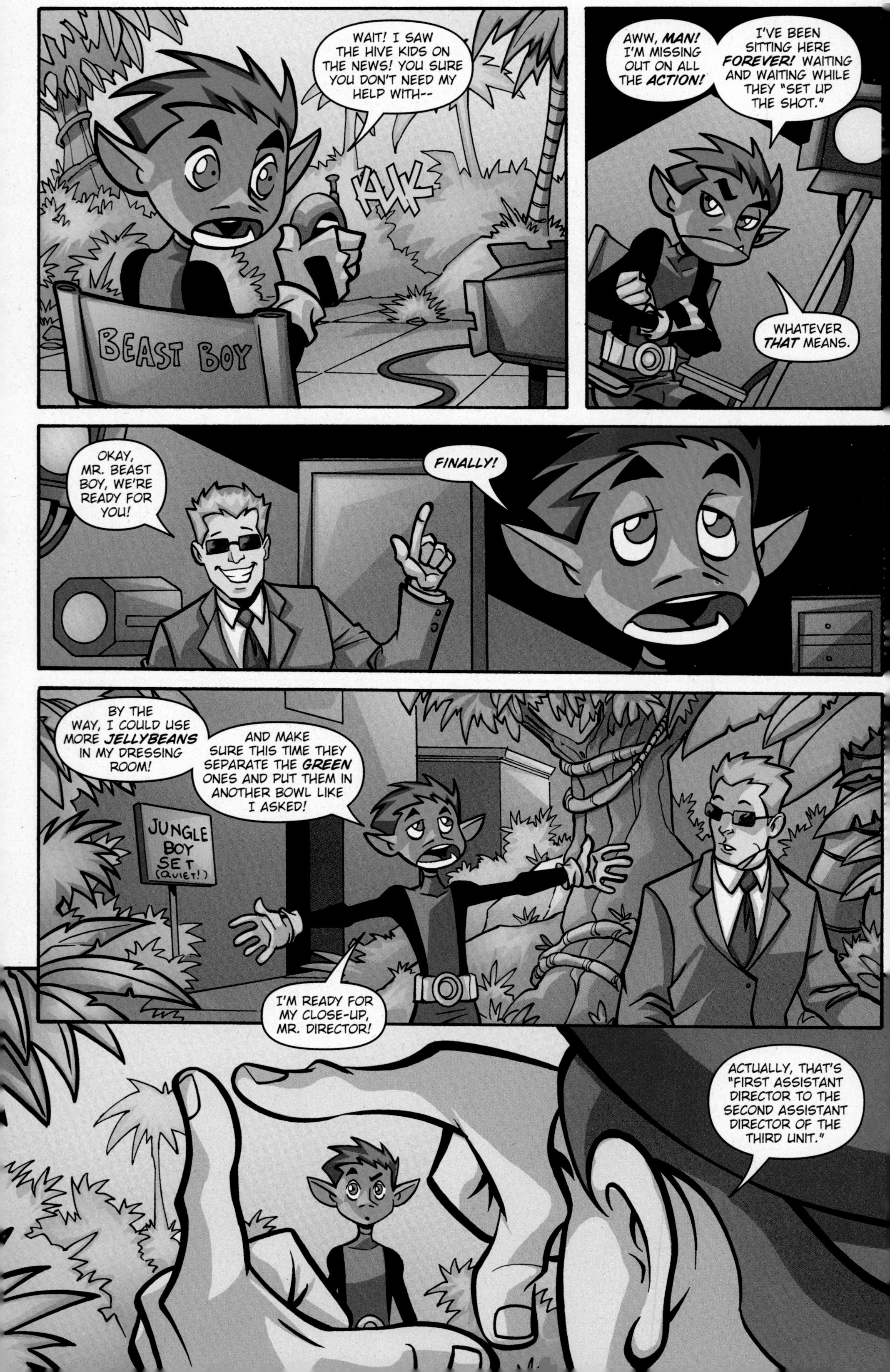

WAIT! I SAW THE HIVE KIDS ON THE NEWS! YOU SURE YOU DON'T NEED MY HELP WITH--
KLIK
BEAST BOY

AWW, *MAN!* I'M MISSING OUT ON ALL THE *ACTION!*
I'VE BEEN SITTING HERE *FOREVER!* WAITING AND WAITING WHILE THEY "SET UP THE SHOT."
WHATEVER *THAT* MEANS.

OKAY, MR. BEAST BOY, WE'RE READY FOR YOU!
FINALLY!

BY THE WAY, I COULD USE MORE ***JELLYBEANS*** IN MY DRESSING ROOM!

AND MAKE SURE THIS TIME THEY SEPARATE THE ***GREEN*** ONES AND PUT THEM IN ANOTHER BOWL LIKE I ASKED!

JUNGLE BOY SET (QUIET!)

I'M READY FOR MY CLOSE-UP, MR. DIRECTOR!

ACTUALLY, THAT'S "FIRST ASSISTANT DIRECTOR TO THE SECOND ASSISTANT DIRECTOR OF THE THIRD UNIT."

ANYWAY, IN THIS SCENE, ALL WE NEED YOU TO DO IS TURN INTO A LION AND THEN ROAR AT SAFARI GIRL OVER THERE...
"TURN INTO A LION"? "ROAR" AT THE GIRL? BUT I THOUGHT I WAS THE HERO, SO WHY--
OH, YOU'RE OUR HERO ALL RIGHT! BABY, YOU'RE SINGLE-HANDEDLY SAVING THIS PRODUCTION!
I DON'T UNDERSTAND, BUT WHATEVER YOU SAY...
HERE.
WHAT'S THIS?
BREATH MINT. WE ARE SO NOT DOING THIS SCENE UNTIL YOU HAVE ONE.
WHY? DO WE KISS IN THIS SCENE?
AS IF!
OKAY, EVERYONE, QUIET ON THE SET...
READY, KIDS?
AAAND...
GRRAH!

...ACTION!
GRRRAAR!
GRRRAAR!
OH, BE QUIET, YOU BIG APE.
YOU'RE EVEN MORE OBNOXIOUS THAN BEAST BOY.
LET'S SEE HOW *YOU* LIKE BEING CAGED YOURSELF...
BLOOP
FIGURES... DISTRACTED BY BEAST BOY EVEN WHEN HE'S NOT AROUND!

THAT'S IT, BEAST BOY! FREE SAFARI GIRL!

HANG ON, RAY! I'LL HAVE YOU FREE IN A MINUTE!

ARE YOU *GETTING* THIS? I HOPE YOU'RE GETTING ALL OF THIS!

I'VE GOT YOU, STARFIRE!
I HOPE BEAST BOY IS FARING BETTER THAN WE ARE!

LOVE SCENE

GREAT WORK SO FAR, KID! YOU'RE A NATURAL! YOU COULD GO VERY FAR IN THIS BUSINESS!
I KNOW, THANKS! BUT...WHEN DO I GET TO DO SOME ACTUAL ACTING? ALL I'VE BEEN DOING IS... PERFORMING ANIMAL TRICKS!
YEAH, LIKE I SAID, YOU SAVED THIS PRODUCTION, BABY!
WE WERE OVER BUDGET AND COULDN'T AFFORD TO HIRE ALL THE TRAINED ANIMALS THAT WE NEEDED, BUT THEN ALONG CAME BEAST BOY!
OKAY, NEXT I NEED YOU TO TURN INTO AN ALLIGATOR FOR THE EXCITING WRESTLING SCENE IN THE SWAMP!
IT'S A CLASSIC STRUGGLE! MAN VERSUS NATURE! YOU VERSUS JUNGLE BOY!
ME VERSUS JUNGLE BOY? BUT I THOUGHT... I WAS PLAYING JUNGLE BOY... I THOUGHT I WAS THE STAR OF THE MOVIE...
BEAST BOY, MEET CRAIG SNIPES, STAR OF JUNGLE BOY!
UM...ACTUALLY, I'M JUST, LIKE, HIS STUNT DOUBLE. HE'S IN, LIKE, AFRICA FILMING WITH THE FIRST ASSISTANT DIRECTOR AND THE SECOND UNIT.
OR MAYBE IT WAS, LIKE, THE SECOND ASSISTANT DIRECTOR AND THE FIRST UNIT...
AWW, YOU MEAN...I DON'T EVEN GET TO MEET THE ACTUAL STAR OF THE MOVIE?!

ONE...
...TWO...
...THREE...
...FOUR...
...FIVE!
LOOKS LIKE THE HIVE FIVE HAS YOU OUTNUMBERED!
YOU'VE BEEN UNSUCCESSFUL-- EMPHASIS ON THE "SUCK"--TRYING TO STOP US SO FAR. WHAT MAKES YOU THINK TODAY WILL BE ANY DIFFERENT?
A WISE MAN ONCE SAID...

...THAT THE WORLD IS LIKE A *MOVIE* AND WE'RE ALL JUST *ACTORS!*
WE EACH HAVE OUR PARTS TO PLAY, AND RIGHT NOW, I'VE BEEN CAST IN THE SUPPORTING ROLE OF A *TEEN TITAN!*
IT MAY NOT WIN ME ANY AWARDS, BUT IT'S THE MOST IMPORTANT ROLE OF MY CAREER!
WHAT WAS *THAT* ABOUT?
IT SOUNDED GOOD WHEN I REHEARSED IT IN MY HEAD.
GLAD TO HAVE YOU BACK, B! YOU CAN TEEL US ALL ABOUT TINSELTOWN LATER. BUT NOW THAT IT'S FIVE AGAINST FIVE...
TEEN TITANS... GO!
KNOCK KNOCK!
WHO'S THERE?
OLIVER!
OLIVER WHO?
OLIVER BUT THE CRYING!

A FEW MONTHS LATER...
LOOK WHAT WE FOUND AT "DISCOUNT DVD WORLD"!
COULD IT BE? IS THAT THE "JUNGLE BOY"!-- THE BUSTER BLOCKING FEATURE FILM STARRING OUR VERY OWN BEAST BOY?
JUNGLE BOY
IT ACTUALLY WENT STRAIGHT TO VIDEO, DIRECT TO DVD...
WELL, THAT DIDN'T TAKE LONG.
WHEN DID YOU MAKE THAT MOVIE AGAIN? WASN'T IT AROUND THE TIME WE PUT THE HIVE FIVE IN JAIL?
THEN AGAIN, IT TOOK THEM EVEN LESS TIME TO BREAK OUT...
SO, WHAT DO YOU THINK WILL HAPPEN *FIRST?* WE TANGLE WITH THE HIVE FIVE AGAIN...OR BEAST BOY GETS ANOTHER PART IN A MOVIE?
WHAT ARE YOU DOING, STARFIRE?
I AM INITIATING THE FAST FORWARD! I CANNOT WAIT TO SEE A SCENE IN WHICH BEAST BOY APPEARS!

HUH...THERE DOES NOT SEEM TO BE ANY BEAST BOY TO BE SEEN... ARE YOU CERTAIN THIS IS THE RIGHT MOVIE?
WAIT A MINUTE! PAUSE IT RIGHT THERE!
THAT'S SUPPOSED TO BE ME!
BUT, BEAST BOY, THAT LION IS NOT GREEN!
OH NO THEY DIDN'T!
DUDE! THEY DIGITALLY COLORED ME! THEY USED SPECIAL EFFECTS TO MAKE ALL THE ANIMALS THEIR NATURAL COLOR!
THERE'S NO WAY PEOPLE ARE GONNA EVEN KNOW THAT'S ME!
AND BY PEOPLE YOU MEAN THE THRONGS OF FANS RUSHING THE BARGAIN BINS FOR THEIR COPY OF "JUNGLE BOY"?
NO, I MEAN PEOPLE LIKE THE CASTING DIRECTOR OF THE NEW "BEAST BUY" PET STORE COMMERCIAL!
I'VE GOT AN AUDITION THIS AFTERNOON!

FEBRUARY 12TH.
CYBORG!
ROBIN
STARFIRE
RAVEN
BEAST BOY
AAARGH!!!
LOVE IS A BATTLEFIELD

TITANS... GO!
BUT DON'T--
AAAAH!
KRZZZZT
WAAAAAH!
ZZZZZT
--TOUCH CYBORG!

AZARATH...
METRION...
...ZINTHOS!
FFFSHHH
HSSSSSS
IS EVERYONE -KOFF- ALL RIGHT? -KOFF-
I AM IN... SATISFACTORY CONDITION.
WHAT HAPPENED TO OVERLOAD?
HE SEEMS TO HAVE DISAPPEARED...THE WATER DISPELLED HIS ENERGY AND IT LOOKS LIKE HE...EVAPORATED INTO STEAM!
HEY, CYBORG... ARE YOU OKAY?
CYBORG.
OKAY.
BZT BZT

FEBRUARY 13TH.
WELL, LOOK WHO'S FINALLY AWAKE!
WHERE YOU BEEN ALL MORNING, DUDE? HIDING FROM ME? AVOIDING A REMATCH? SCARED I'M GONNA KICK YOUR BUTT AGAIN?
KICK.
YOUR.
BUTT.
SLO-BO'S
MST3K
WHACK
OWW... THAT HURT!
LOOKS LIKE SOMEONE WOKE UP ON THE WRONG SIDE OF THE BED TODAY.
I KNOW AN ACTIVITY THAT MIGHT HELP THEM RISE FROM THE CORRECT SIDE OF THEIR BED!
STARFIRE'S ARTS & KRAFTS CRAFTS

SHE'S BROKEN OUT THE ARTS AND CRAFTS BOX.
HOW MANY TIMES DO I HAVE TO TELL HER MACARONI IS FOR EATING, NOT GLUING ON EMPTY TOILET PAPER ROLLS TO MAKE PENCIL HOLDERS!
OH... IS THAT WHAT THAT WAS?
STARFIRE'S ARTS & KRAFTS CRAFTS
I AM CERTAIN THAT WE ALL REMEMBER WHAT DAY IT IS TOMORROW...
...THEREFORE I THOUGHT WE MIGHT PARTAKE IN AN ARTISTIC GROUP PROJECT IN PREPARATION FOR--
ALL RIGHT, GUYS, I'M OFF!
SEE YOU IN A FEW DAYS. CALL ME ON THE T-COMMUNICATOR IF THERE'S AN EMERGENCY.
R-ROBIN, WHERE ARE Y-YOU GOING?
TO THE KYODO-HAN TEMPLE TO TRAIN WITH THE TRUE MASTER, REMEMBER?
BUT... BUT...

...TOMORROW IS THE DAY OF THE VALENTINES!
UM... OH, YEAH...
SO IT IS...
WELL, YOU GUYS HAVE FUN! SAVE ME SOME CHOCOLATES. SEE YOU ON--
KLONK
WHAT?
IT IS... THAT IS...I THOUGHT WE MIGHT...
...NOTHING.
BE SAFE ON YOUR JOURNEY TO THE TEMPLE. AND GOOD LUCK WITH YOUR TRAINING.
KNOCK-KNOCK
WHO'S THERE?
CUPID.
CUPID WHO?
CUPID THOSE CHOCOLATES CLOSER TO ME!

SO, UH, FRIENDS...
OH-NO, SHE'S BUSTING OUT THE FACE...
...MIGHT YOU BE INTERESTED IN CREATING THE TRADITIONAL VALENTINES CARDS WITH THE LACE AND THE PAINT OF GLITTER...
MOVE: WET EYES
HP DAMAGE:-125
MP DAMAGE:-150
MOVE: QUIVERING LIPS
HP DAMAGE:-100
MP DAMAGE:-125
MUST...NOT... MAKE...EYE CONTACT...
...AND EXCHANGING THEM TOMORROW OVER HEART-SHAPED CHOCOLATES AND CANDIES WITH WRITTEN SENTIMENTS ON THEM SUCH AS "BE MINE" AND "I...I...I LOVE YOU."
MUST... RESIST...THE FACE...
MOVE: FORLORN FACE
HP DAMAGE:-175
MP DAMAGE:-200
MOVE: HEART SHIELD
HP DAMAGE:-200
MP DAMAGE:-250
AS MUCH AS I LOVE GETTING ALL CRAFTY, I'VE ALREADY MADE PLANS AND I, UH, HAVE TO GO AND, UM, CONFIRM THOSE PLANS... RIGHT NOW!
YEAH, AND YOU KNOW HOW MUCH I LOVE THE GLITTER, BUT I'M, UH, BUSY TOMORROW...AND WILL YOU LOOK AT THE TIME! I'M LATE FOR MY APPOINTMENT WITH THE VET!
MOVE: HUG OF DOOM
HP DAMAGE:-300
MP DAMAGE:-500

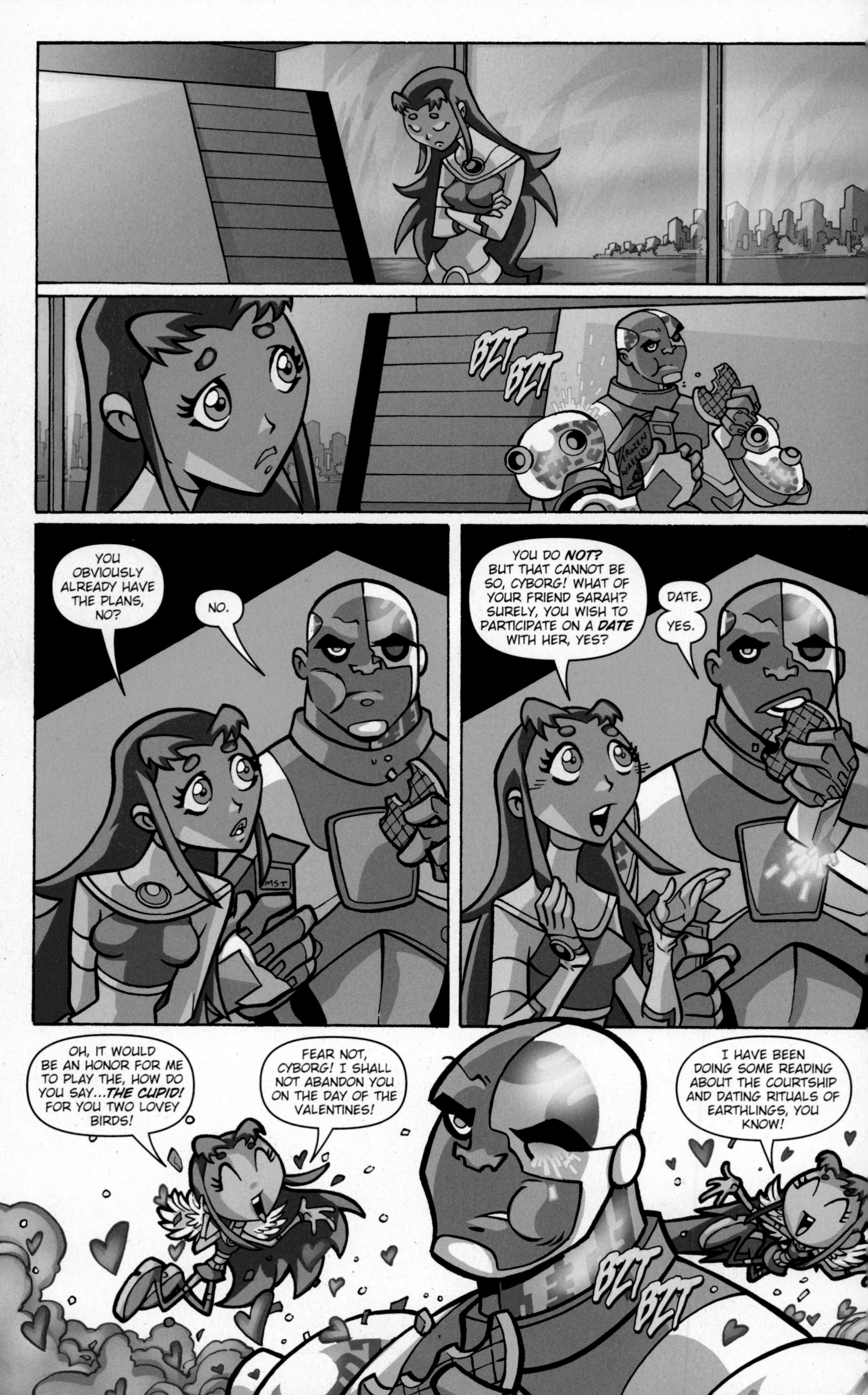
BZZT
BZZT
YOU OBVIOUSLY ALREADY HAVE THE PLANS, NO?
NO.
YOU DO NOT? BUT THAT CANNOT BE SO, CYBORG! WHAT OF YOUR FRIEND SARAH? SURELY, YOU WISH TO PARTICIPATE ON A DATE WITH HER, YES?
DATE.
YES.
OH, IT WOULD BE AN HONOR FOR ME TO PLAY THE, HOW DO YOU SAY...THE CUPID! FOR YOU TWO LOVEY BIRDS!
FEAR NOT, CYBORG! I SHALL NOT ABANDON YOU ON THE DAY OF THE VALENTINES!
I HAVE BEEN DOING SOME READING ABOUT THE COURTSHIP AND DATING RITUALS OF EARTHLINGS, YOU KNOW!
BZZT
BZZT

FEBRUARY 14TH.
TO: CYBORG
FROM: A SECRET ADMIRER
I'LL JUST LEAVE THIS RIGHT HERE FOR--
HEY! THAT'S HIS CAR HYRDOPLANING ACROSS THE WATER!
NOW, WHERE COULD HE BE OFF TO?
TODAY'S VALENTINE'S DAY BUT HE BETTER NOT BE DOING WHAT I THINK HE'S DOING...

SARAH SHOULD BE HERE MOMENTARILY!
I HOPE SHE APPROVES OF THE EATERY I HAVE CHOSEN FOR YOUR DATE. ANYWAY, I SHALL BE RIGHT HERE SO AS NOT TO BE A WHEEL OF THE THIRD KIND...ENJOY YOURSELVES BUT CALL IF YOU NEED ME!
CYBORG! HI, THERE!
!
I BROUGHT YOU SOMETHING! HAPPY VALENTINE'S DAY!
BZT
BZT
GASP!
I HAVE FAILED CYBORG! I HAVE FORGOTTEN THE FLOWERS AND THE CHOCOLATES! I AM THE WORST CUPID EVER!
SO...HOW HAVE YOU BEEN? HAVEN'T SEEN OR HEARD FROM YOU IN A WHILE. GUESS THE TITANS ARE KEEPING YOU BUSY--
AHEM.

HELLO, MY NAME IS JINX AND I'LL BE YOUR SERVER TODAY.
CAN I START YOU OFF WITH SOME DRINKS?
WHAT ARE YOU DOING HERE?!
I WAS ABOUT TO ASK CYBORG AND THIS...THIS...HUSSY THE SAME THING!
HER NAME IS NOT "HUSSY"-- IT IS SARAH!
BOFF
UM...MIGHT I SUGGEST YOU TWO POSTPONE YOUR BONDING OVER FOODS UNTIL AFTER THE ENJOYMENT OF A SHARED MOVIE EXPERIENCE PERHAPS?
I SHALL TAKE CARE OF THIS JINX...

UM...YOU HAD STARFIRE CALL ME AND MAKE THE RESERVATIONS AND EVERYTHING, BUT DON'T TELL ME SHE'S ALSO HERE TO, LIKE, CHAPERONE US!
GO AHEAD, YOU TWO! RUN ALONG NOW AND BE LOVING!
SHHING
MIGHT I SUGGEST THE HOLDING OF THE HANDS AND--
OOF!

NOW, SEE HERE, VILLAINESS...
SHHING
YOU ARE RUINING THE ROMANTIC PLANS I HAVE MADE FOR CYBORG AND SARAH!
IF WE ARE DONE HERE, I SHALL CONTINUE MY DUTIES AS THE CUPID AND SALVAGE WHAT I CAN OF THIS DATE...
SHE'S PLAYING CUPID FOR CYBORG?!
WHY, I OUGHTA...
WELL, DO NOT JUST STAND THERE, LOVEY BIRDS!

THE JUMP CITY STAR GIVES ***THIS*** FEATURE "TWO UPS OF THE THUMB" AND THE GOTHAM GAZETTE CALLS IT "THE PERFECT DATE MOVIE."

UM...OKAY, BUT WHAT ABOUT JINX? MAYBE YOU TWO SHOULD JUST GO AND DO YOUR SUPERHERO THING...CYBORG SEEMS PREOCCUPIED ANYWAY...

I KNOW YOU MEAN WELL, STARFIRE, BUT MAYBE HE DOESN'T REALLY WANT TO BE HERE...MAYBE THIS DATE WASN'T SUCH A GOOD IDEA...

OH, NO, NO! HE MOST ***CERTAINLY*** WISHES TO BE HERE!

BUT HE'S BARELY SAID A ***WORD*** TO ME! AND HE'S ACTING REALLY WEIRD! ALMOST LIKE A ***ROBOT!***

NO WAY!
HE GAVE HER FLOWERS?!
HE NEVER GAVE ME FLOWERS!
ZZAPP
HEE-HEE-HEE!
YOU WILL NOT TURN THIS DATE INTO A ROMANTIC COMEDY!

UM, LISTEN...CYBORG...I'M NOT SURE EXACTLY WHAT'S GOING ON HERE, BUT I CAN TELL THAT SOMETHING'S WRONG...
YOU HAVEN'T REALLY CALLED IN A WHILE...AND I DON'T EVEN REMEMBER THE LAST TIME WE HUNG OUT...
MAYBE YOU'VE BEEN BUSY...I MEAN, I KNOW THE SONG "HEROES ON PATROL" AND ALL THAT...MAYBE YOU'VE BEEN IN OUTER SPACE AGAIN...OR...MAYBE YOU'VE JUST LOST INTEREST IN ME...
...AND MAYBE JINX OVER THERE HAS SOMETHING TO DO WITH IT.
BZT BZT

WHY ARE YOU DOING THIS, JINX? WHY DO YOU SABOTAGE THE DAY OF THE VALENTINES FOR CYBORG?

AS IF YOU DON'T KNOW! LIKE HE DIDN'T TELL YOU ABOUT US AND WHAT HAPPENED WHEN HE WAS A STUDENT AT THE H.I.V.E. ACADEMY!

YOU SPEAK OF THE TIME CYBORG WAS THE SPY AT YOUR EVIL SCHOOL OF VILLAINOUS TEACHINGS?

BUT HE HAS ***NEVER*** SPOKEN OF YOU OR ANYTHING OUT OF THE ORDINARY THAT MIGHT HAVE TRANSPIRED BETWEEN THE TWO OF YOU!
WHAT?!

I HATE BOYS!
SEE THE EPISODE: "DECEPTION"

SO, YOU NEVER TOLD YOUR FRIENDS ABOUT US, HUH?
WHY'S THAT? WERE YOU EMBARRASSED OF ME?
EMBARRASSED THAT I DON'T MEASURE UP TO THEIR GOODY-GOODY STANDARDS?
SHREEE
CYBORG! LOOK OUT!
KLANG
FFFSHHHHHT
RRRRARGH!
KRZZT KRZZZT
CYBORG!

Huff
Puff
O-OVERLOAD?!
BUT I THOUGHT RAVEN SAID HE HAD... "EVAPORTATED"?
NO, HE ESCAPED...BY HIDING INSIDE OF ME...POSSESSING ME LIKE AN EVIL SPIRIT...
LIKE A GHOST IN THE MACHINE !
I'VE BEEN FIGHTING HIM THIS WHOLE TIME, TRYING TO GET HIM OUT...
CYBORG! LOOK OUT!
DON'T YOU DARE LAY A HAND ON HIM!
SHREE
SHREE

JINX! WHAT'S SHE DOING HERE?
SHE SAVED YOU, CYBORG.
SARAH! WHAT'S GOING ON HERE?
I'VE BEEN LOST INSIDE OF MY OWN HEAD ALL THIS TIME, TRYING TO KEEP OVERLOAD FROM TAKING OVER MY SYSTEM, MY BODY, MY...LIFE!
CYBORG...I'VE BEEN THINKING...MAYBE WE SHOULD STOP SEEING EACH OTHER...YOU'RE WAY TOO BUSY WITH ALL THESE SUPER VILLAINS TO EVEN CALL AND...IT'S GETTING KINDA DANGEROUS FOR ME TO BE AROUND YOU!
SO... TAKE CARE, OKAY?
WAIT! SARAH...
I CAN EXPLAIN WHY I HAVEN'T CALLED!
AND WOULD YOU CARE TO EXPLAIN EXACTLY WHAT WENT ON BETWEEN YOU AND JINX?
WHY DID YOU NOT TELL ANY OF YOUR FRIENDS--NOT EVEN ME--ABOUT IT? ARE ALL EARTH BOYS EMOTIONALLY CHALLENGED?!
ULP.
NOTHING REALLY HAPPENED BETWEEN ME AND JINX! NOTHING SERIOUS, AT LEAST!
COME ON, GIRLS, I CAN EXPLAIN EVERYTHING!
COME BACK TO CY-BABY!
END

ROBIN

RAVEN

STARFIRE

CYBORG

SO, I TURNED TO HIM, LOOKED HIM STERNLY IN THE EYE AND SAID...

BEAST BOY

MENTO

NEGATIVE MAN

ELASTI-GIRL

ROBOTMAN

SURPRISES

The Watering Hole of Ev
ARE YOU A MAN OR A MOUSE, BEAST BOY?
SQUEAK SQUEAK
THAT RESPONSE IS AS UNACCEPTABLE AS IT IS UNAMUSING.
NOW BE A GOOD LITTLE SOLDIER, GET IN THERE, AND STICK TO THE BATTLE PLAN!
Y-YES, SIR!

WELL, WELL, WELL...
...WHAT HAVE WE HERE?
HAS THE DOOM PATROL'S LITTLE MASCOT LOST HIS WAY?
DOOM PATROL...

...ATTACK!
AND THAT'S HOW WE LURED MADAME ROUGE OUT OF HIDING AND CAPTURED HER.
WHAT'S THE MATTER, ROBIN? YOU LOOKED ALMOST AS SURPRISED AS ROUGE DID...

UH...YOU USED BEAST BOY AS BAIT?!
THE MAN IS OBVIOUSLY A TACTICAL GENIUS.
YOU'RE A GOOD LEADER, ROBIN. ONE DAY YOU COULD BE A GREAT LEADER--IF YOU LEARN TO TAKE CONTROL OF YOUR TEAM, FULLY EXPLOIT ITS STRENGTHS, NOT LET ANY WEAKNESSES SLOW YOU DOWN...
...AND DO A LITTLE GROWING UP YOURSELF.
TWITCH
THAT WAS ONE OF OUR EARLIEST ENCOUNTERS WITH MADAME ROUGE. BEAST BOY WAS UNSURE AND FEARFUL BACK THEN, SO HE NEEDED TO FACE HIS FEARS IF HE WAS EVER TO OVERCOME THEM.
BUT...WAS HE NOT...A MERE CHILD AT THE TIME?
HE WAS A MEMBER OF THE "DOOM" PATROL, NOT THE "DAYCARE" PATROL. NO ONE EVER SAID OUR LINE OF WORK WAS EASY, AND WHEN DUTY CALLS--

I WANNA HEAR MORE STORIES ABOUT "BABY BEAST BOY"!
LET ME JUST FIND A PLACE TO PUT THESE THINGS...
HUH. THAT'S A LOT OF PRESENTS.
THIS BIG ONE'S FROM TITANS EAST. THEY'RE OFF ON A MISSION SO THEY COULDN'T MAKE IT.
THAT ONE OVER THERE WAS SENT BY THUNDER AND LIGHTNING...AND HOTSPOT DROPPED HIS OFF IN CASE HE WAS LATE 'CAUSE HIS THERAPY SESSION WENT LONG...AND KID FLASH SAID HE'D BE BY--
I HOPE FOR YOUR SAKE NONE OF THESE ARE TOOLS OF ANY KIND!
MY SAKE? WHAT DO YOU MEAN?
YOU KNOW HOW EVERY KID GOES THROUGH A "BUILDING PHASE"?
DID YOU HEAR THE ONE ABOUT THE MUMMY WHO WAS SO VAIN THAT HE WAS ALL WRAPPED UP IN HIMSELF?
WHO'RE YOU CALLING A MUMMY? WAIT, WHO'RE YOU CALLING VAIN?

"BEAST BOY WAS NO DIFFERENT...
"IT STARTED WITH BLOCKS AND TOYS LIKE THAT.
"THEN HE STARTED STACKING ANYTHING HE COULD GET HIS HANDS ON..."
HIGHER, RITA! HIGHER!
"...AND MADE ME HELP HIM!
"WHEN HE GOT TIRED OF BUILDING STUFF UP, HE STARTED TAKING OBJECTS APART.
"EVEN AFTER GETTING IN TROUBLE FOR DISASSEMBLING THINGS HE SHOULDN'T HAVE...
"...HIS CURIOSITY GOT THE BETTER OF HIM AND HE JUST HAD TO SEE THE INSIDES OF EVERYTHING AND CHECK OUT WHAT THEY WERE MADE OF."

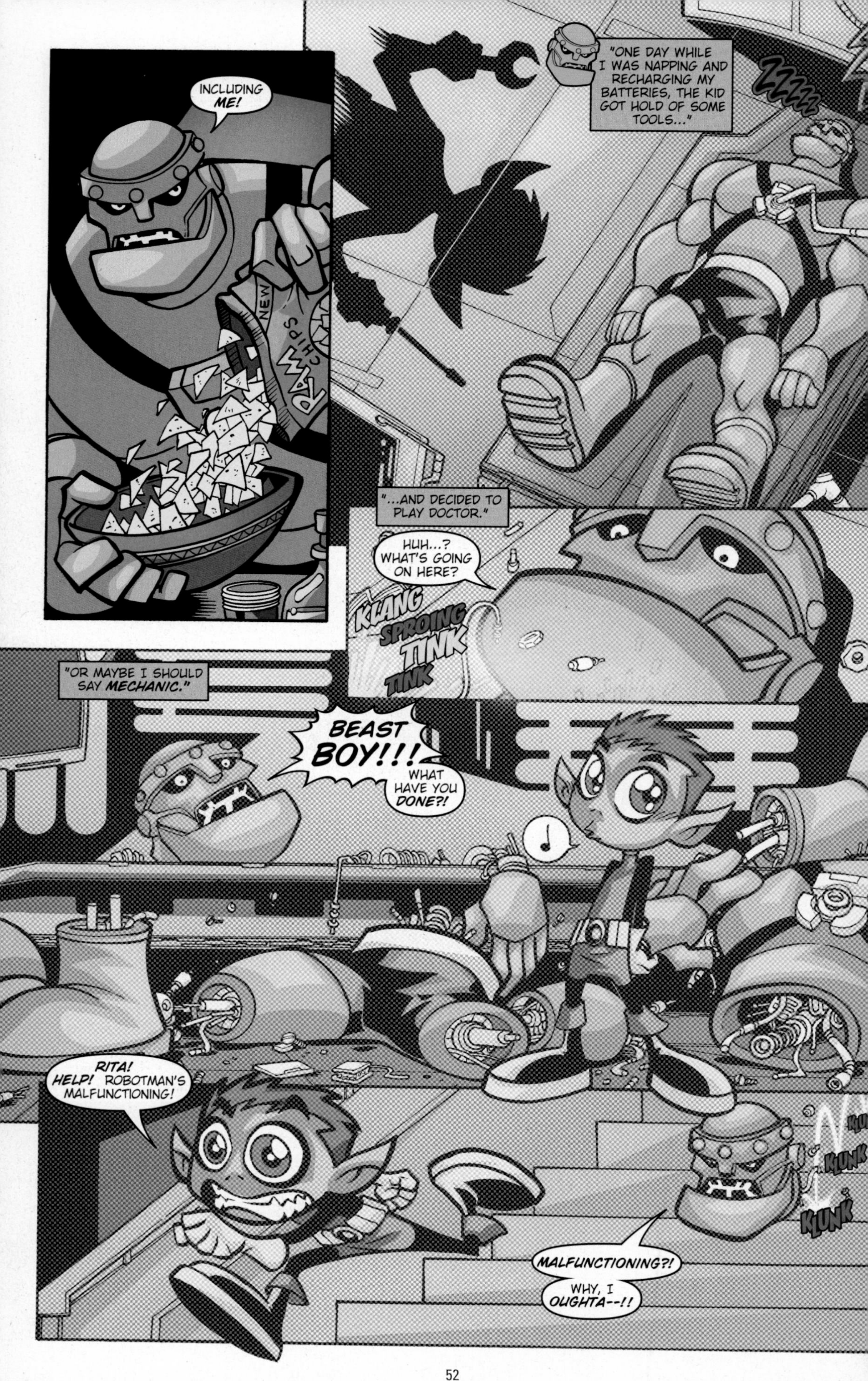

INCLUDING ME!
NEW
RAMS CHIPS
"ONE DAY WHILE I WAS NAPPING AND RECHARGING MY BATTERIES, THE KID GOT HOLD OF SOME TOOLS..."
ZZZZZ
"...AND DECIDED TO PLAY DOCTOR."
HUH...? WHAT'S GOING ON HERE?
KLANG
SPROING
TINK
TINK
"OR MAYBE I SHOULD SAY MECHANIC."
BEAST BOY!!!
WHAT HAVE YOU DONE?!
RITA! HELP! ROBOTMAN'S MALFUNCTIONING!
KLUNK
KLUNK
MALFUNCTIONING?!
WHY, I OUGHTA--!!

I HAVE TO ADMIT I WAS A BIT HARD ON THE LITTLE RUNT. NO REAL DAMAGE WAS DONE AND STEVE PUT ME BACK TOGETHER, BUT...
...WE NEVER DID FIGURE OUT WHERE THIS THING GOES!
I DIDN'T THINK YOU WERE HARD ENOUGH, CLIFF.
OH, STEVE, AFTER ALL OF THAT HE DID LEARN TO BETTER RESPECT OTHER PEOPLE'S SPACE AND PROPERTY.
COULD'VE FOOLED ME.
SO, B.B. WAS ALWAYS A BIT OF A "SCREW UP," HUH?
GOOD ONE, CYBORG.
SNICKER
I DO NOT GET IT...
THERE WERE TIMES WHEN HE DID GOOD, OF COURSE.
REMEMBER WHEN HE FIRST FOUGHT THE ANIMAL-VEGETABLE-MINERAL MAN?
ANIMAL...
...VEGETABLE...
...MINERAL...
...MAN?

SUPERMAN
DC
NATIONAL COMICS
12¢
Introducing "THE DOOM PATROL"
MY GREATEST ADVENTURE
"YES, BEAST BOY WAS QUITE FRIGHTENED OF HIM...
"IF YOU EVER SAW THE ANIMAL-VEGETABLE-MINERAL MAN, YOU'D UNDERSTAND *WHY!*"

"WE HIT THAT THING..."
WHOOOM WHOOOM WHOOOM
"...WITH EVERYTHING WE HAD!
SHHHOOM
"IT CAME BACK AT US..."
HOLD YOUR POSITION, CLIFF!
RRRARGH!
"...WITH EVERYTHING *IT* HAD!"
M-MY LEG...I'M ***TRAPPED!***
WHAM

"AS IF BEAST BOY WASN'T TERRIFIED ENOUGH...
"...HE THEN HAD TO WITNESS THIS GRUESOME CREATURE GIVE HIS FAMILY A SOUND BEATING!
"BUT WHEN HE SAW US HURT LIKE THAT...
"...HE SPRANG INTO ACTION!
"...WITHOUT FURTHER HESITATION...
KRRRRAK
KRRRRAK
"...AND WITHOUT ANY ORDERS OR EVEN A SINGLE WORD FROM MENTO!"

I WAS SO *PROUD* OF HIM THAT DAY.
AND THAT WAS JUST THE FIRST OF A HANDFUL OF TIMES THAT GREEN BEAN SAVED OUR HIDES.
ADMIT IT, YOU WERE PROUD OF HIM THAT DAY, TOO.
LA-REEE...
WOW, COMPARED TO THIS DUDE, RAVEN'S "MISS WARM 'N' FUZZY"...
WHAT'S THAT SUPPOSED TO MEAN!

ALL RIGHT, WE'VE GOT PLENTY OF OUR OWN BEAST-BOY-AS-HERO MEMORIES, SO HOW ABOUT GIVING US MORE ***"EMBARRASSMENT AMMO"!***

WELL, THERE WAS THAT VERY FIRST TRAINING SESSION WHEN STEVE TRIED TO COACH HIM INTO TRANSFORMING INTO ***BIGGER*** ANIMALS...

LOOK, SQUIRRELS AND DOGS AND MONKEYS ARE FINE, BEAST BOY...

...BUT YOU NEED TO THINK "BIGGER."

YES, SIR!

NOT BAD, SON. BUT THINK EVEN "BIGGER."

SIR, YES, SIR!

WELL, YOU HAVE TO ADMIT HE ***IS*** BIGGER!

HA! THAT'S PRETTY FUNNY! AND KINDA CUTE.
WELL, IF YOU WANT CUTE STORIES--
OH, I DON'T KNOW IF I SHOULD BE TELLING YOU THIS...
PRAY TELL US, ELASTI-GIRL! TELL US! TELL US!
OH, ALL RIGHT...
ONE OF GARFIELD'S ALL-TIME FAVORITE FAIRY TALES WAS "THE FROG PRINCE."
NOCK-NOCK!
WHO'S THERE?
RITA!
RITA WHO?
RITA BOOK! YOU MIGHT LEARN SOMETHING!

"HE JUST LOVED HOW THE FROG TRANSFORMED INTO PRINCE CHARMING...
"...WITH A KISS FROM A FAIR MAIDEN."
AND ON SOME NIGHTS WHEN I'D TELL HIM IT WAS BEDTIME, HE'D TURN INTO A FROG...
"...AND REFUSE TO GO TO HIS ROOM!
"...SO I'D HAVE TO PICK HIM UP, CARRY HIM TO HIS BED, KISS HIM GOOD NIGHT, AND SAY:
"'GOOD NIGHT, PRINCE CHARMING.'"
THEN HE'D CHANGE BACK AND REPLY, "GOOD NIGHT, FAIR MAIDEN" AND FINALLY GO TO SLEEP...
AWWW, HOW SIMPLY PRECIOUS!

YOU BABIED HIM TOO MUCH, RITA.
AND YOU WERE TOO **STRICT** WITH HIM.
THE BOY NEEDED DISCIPLINE AND DIRECTION.
HE ALSO NEEDED SOME AFFIRMATION, AND A LITTLE AFFECTION WOULDN'T HAVE HURT.
I HATE IT WHEN "MOMMY" AND "DADDY" FIGHT.
I UNDERSTAND WHERE YOU'RE COMING FROM, MENTO. BUT TRUST ME, I KNOW WHAT BEAST BOY WENT THROUGH. AND WITH ALL DUE RESPECT, LEAVING HIS MENTOR AND JOINING THE TITANS HAS BEEN A GOOD THING FOR HIM.
FOR BOTH OF US.
YEAH, AND WE DON'T MAKE HIM WEAR THAT SILLY MASK.
HOLD.
IT.
RIGHT.
THERE.

WHEW!
THE MASK WAS *HIS* IDEA!
SO, NO ONE MADE HIM WEAR THAT STUPID MASK? IT WAS HIS CHOICE?
YUP.
HE THOUGHT IT MADE HIM LOOK *"MYSTERIOUS."*
I THOUGHT HE LOOKED CUTE!
YES, IT WAS HIS CHOICE, JUST LIKE THE ABORTED GUITAR LESSONS, KARATE CLASSES, BOY SCOUTS, AND THAT PUPPY HE BEGGED US TO GET HIM...
...BUT GUESS WHO HAD TO PICK WHO UP FROM CAMP IN THE MIDDLE OF THE NIGHT, NOT TO MENTION PICK UP AFTER "CHIEF" ALL THE TIME!

OKAY, SO WE KNOW WHERE THE MASK CAME FROM...BUT WHO WANTS TO TELL US WHERE BEAST BOY GOT A DORKY NAME LIKE "GARFIELD"?
YEAH, WHAT'S UP WITH THAT?
I MUST ADMIT THAT EVEN BY THE STANDARDS OF THE EARTH AND ITS ODDLY NAMED ANIMALS CALLED "MOOSE" AND MEN WHO ANSWER TO "TOM," A NAME SUCH AS "GARFIELD" BRINGS THE MOST AMUSEMENT TO MY EARS!
WHO IN THEIR RIGHT MIND WOULD NAME THEIR KID "GARFIELD"?
AND EXACTLY WHAT'S WRONG WITH THE NAME "GARFIELD"?
HEY!
B-BEAST BOY... YOU'RE HOME... EARLY.
ER...HIYA... SQUIRT.

WHAT ARE YOU GUYS DOING HERE?
WELL, YOU SEE... THE PARTOL OF DOOM ARE HERE TO...THAT IS TO SAY...
SURPRISE!
HAPPY BIRTHDAY BEAST BOY!
WEE-OOH-WEE-OOH
ALERT
CITY SECTOR
80
UH-OH! PRISON BREAK! THE PARTY'S GONNA HAVE TO WAIT!
BUT...BUT... I SEE CAKE! AND PRESENTS!
LET'S GO, BEAST BOY! DUTY CALLS!
YOU HEARD THE MAN, "PRINCE CHARMING"!
D-DID SHE JUST CALL M-ME..."PRINCE CHARMING"?
AREN'T SURPRISES FUN?
NOT THE END

HEY, CHILDREN!
DO YOU KNOW WHAT TIME IT IS?

IT'S YUMMY YUMMY TIME!
???
GOTH

THAT'S RIGHT!
I'M GUY CRUST, AND THIS IS...
WHAT KIND OF SNAKE IS FOUND IN A BAKERY?

WHO WANTS PIE?
GUEST STARRING BUMBLEBEE!
A PIE-THON!

LET'S MEET OUR CONTESTANTS!
HE'S PART TEEN, PART MACHINE...
...HIS HOBBIES ARE WORKING ON HIS CAR, PLAYING STANKBALL, AND MAKING NEW FRIENDS--ESPECIALLY THE LADIES...
HE'S COME ALL THE WAY FROM JUMP CITY, PLEASE WELCOME...
...CYBORG!
HOW COOL IS THIS! I CAN'T BELIEVE THEY PICKED US!
OUR NEXT CONTESTANT IS ALL TEEN AND ALL GREEN...
...A VEGETARIAN AND ANIMAL LOVER WHOSE HOBBIES ARE PLAYING VIDEO GAMES AND THE TUBORKLE WHEN HE'S NOT PLAYING PRACTICAL JOKES...
HE ALSO HAILS FROM JUMP CITY, LET'S HAVE A BIG HAND FOR...
...BEAST BOY!
TOLD YOU JUMPING UP AND DOWN AND SCREAMING IN LINE WOULD GET US NOTICED!
AND OUR FINAL CONTESTANT IS A NATIVE OF TAMARAN WHO NOW CALLS EARTH HOME...
...SHE ENJOYS COOKING, SINGING AND POETRY, HER FAVORITE HOLIDAY IS BLORTHOG, AND SHE CLAIMS TO LOVE EVERYTHING AND EVERYBODY...
LADIES AND GENTLEMEN, A NICE ROUND OF APPLAUSE FOR...
...STARFIRE!
THE SHOW OF GAMES...YET ANOTHER ODD BUT INTRIGUING PART OF THE EARTH CULTURE...
!
SPOOKS ILLUSTRATED
JAPAN
JAPANESE PHRASES

AND NOW, TELL THEM WHAT THEY'VE WON, CHARLIE!
BEAST BOY, CYBORG, AND STARFIRE, GET READY TO JUMP FOR JOY AND HA-PIE-NESS BECAUSE YOU'VE JUST WON...
A PYRAMID OF PIE!!!
OH MY, GOSH! I CAN'T... I CAN'T BELIEVE IT! I NEVER WIN ANYTHING! THIS IS...THIS IS WICKED AWESOME!
BOO-YA!
BUT... I AM... PERPLEXED.
MUST WE NOT PARTICIPATE AND BE VICTORIOUS IN THE GAMES BEFORE WE ARE AWARDED THE PRIZE?
YES, BUT WHAT TIME IS IT?
UM...I DO NOT HAVE THE WATCH, BUT I BELIEVE IT IS APPROXIMATELY THE HALF PAST THE--
WRONG! TELL HER, CHILDREN...

IT'S YUMMY YUMMY TIME!
EASY THERE, ELBOWS!!!
THAT'S RIGHT, SO HAVE A SLICE!
URK!
MM-MM-MM! DON'T MIND IF I DO!
ARUM NUM NUM NUM
NOW THAT YOU'VE RECEIVED YOUR PRIZE, IT'S TIME FOR YOUR FIRST CHALLENGE!
OH... KAY.
THIS CHALLENGE IS CALLED THE "THREE-LEGGED RACE."
WHICH ONE OF YOU IS GOING TO COMPETE?
OOH, LET'S DO IT! YOU AND ME, B.B.!
YEAH, WE GOT THIS ONE!
SORRY, NO, THIS GAME IS FOR ONE CHALLENGER ONLY.
SAY WHAT? YOU NEED TWO PEOPLE FOR A THREE-LEGGED RACE!
DON'T WORRY, CY! I GOT THIS! I'M THE FASTEST TITAN ANYWAY!
WELL, AFTER KID FLASH... AND MAS Y MENOS...AND MAYBE LIGHTNING...AND AQUALAD IF WE'RE UNDERWATER...ACTUALLY, ROBIN'S GOT THOSE SKINNY BUT MUSCULAR RUNNER'S LEGS...

HEY, ROBIN...
HAVE YOU SEEN BEAST BOY?
SPOOKS ILLUSTRATED
TEMPLES OF JAPAN
JAPANESE PHRASES

HE, CYBORG AND STARFIRE WENT TO THE TAPING OF THAT NEW GAME SHOW.

THAT POINTLESS THING WAS TODAY?
WHY DIDN'T YOU GO? I THOUGHT THEY HAD FOUR TICKETS.

LIKE YOU, RAVEN, I HAD BETTER THINGS TO DO.
SO, THEY TOOK BUMBLEBEE INSTEAD.
MAP OF JAPAN
LUCKY HER.
BROTHERHOOD OF EVIL EXPOSED!
STEAMROLLER STILL AT LARGE
RED X SIGHTING IN STEEL CITY

SO, BEAST BOY, ARE YOU READY TO RUN THE "THREE-LEGGED RACE"?
YEAH, BUT ARE YOU SURE I DON'T NEED A PARTNER...?
NO! ALL YOU NEED IS PIE!
URK!
ARUM NUM NUM NUM
I'M GETTING A WARM AND FUZZY PIE FILLING INSIDE...
POOF!
WHAT THE--?!
AAAAH! I'VE...I'VE GOT THREE LEGS!
OKAY, THAT AIN'T RIGHT!
NO TIME TO FREAK OUT! ONLY TIME TO RUN, BEAST BOY, RUN!

A MAZE! NO FAIR! RUNNING WITH THREE LEGS IS HARD ENOUGH!
START!
HURDLES! DOUBLE NO FAIR!
HURRY! TIME'S RUNNING OUT AND PIE WAITS FOR NO ONE!
FINISH

I –HUFF– DID IT –HUFF– –HUFF–
POOF!
OH, MY! THE MAGIC'S WEARING OFF...
WHAT DID HE JUST SAY?
HEY, CHILDREN! WHAT *TIME* IS IT?
IT'S YUMMY YUMMY TIME!
WHAT'S RAVEN'S FAVORITE PIE?

ROBIN, THIS IS BUMBLEBEE! COME IN!
SOMETHING STRANGE IS GOING ON OVER HERE...
CYBORG, BEAST BOY, AND STARFIRE ARE ACTING REALLY... FLAKY!
I THOUGHT YOU WERE AT A TV SHOW TAPING--
WELL, THIS SHOW'S ALL KINDS OF WEIRD WITH PIE FALLING OUT OF THE SKY AND A HOST USING SOME FUNKY KIND OF MAGIC!
PIE?
MAGIC?
ONLY ONE PERSON COULD BE BEHIND THIS!
KEEP AN EYE ON THINGS, BUMBLEBEE, BUT WAIT FOR BACKUP! WE'RE ON OUR WAY!

IT'S TIME FOR OUR NEXT CHALLENGE, AND SINCE BEAST BOY'S ALREADY HAD A TURN, IT'LL HAVE TO BE ONE-- AND ONLY ONE-- OF YOU...
UH, I DON'T WANT NO THIRD LEG! I JUST WANT PIE!
AND--I DID NOT BRING MY SHOES OF RUNNING BUT THIS PIE IS RATHER TASTY!
NO WORRIES, CHILDREN! IN THIS CHALLENGE ALL YOU HAVE TO DO IS FIND ALL THE VILLAINS ON THIS LIST!
VILLAINS
ADONIS
ATLAS
BRAIN
CONTROL FREAK
JINX
UM, CYBORG SHALL ACCEPT THIS CHALLENGE!
VILLAINS
ME?! WHY ME?
BECAUSE...
...I AM BUSY EATING PIE!
THAT'S THE SPIRIT, TWINKLE STAR!
RASSMFRASSMSTARFIRE
CYBORG, YOUR CHALLENGE BEGINS BEHIND DOOR NUMBER THREE...
3

CIRCLE THE VILLAINS' NAMES IN ANY DIRECTION.

ADONIS • ATLAS • BRAIN • CINDERBLOCK
CONTROL FREAK • JINX • JOHNNY RANCID
KILLER MOTH • MUMBO • OVERLOAD
PLASMUS • PUPPET KING
SEEMORE • SLADE • KATAROU • WARP

```
C K C B R A I N D G U
O A I Y I A P H I G S
N T N M O D L T C N T
T A D S H O A O N I D
R R E A E N S M A K A
O O R L R I M R R T O
L U B T M S U E Y E L
F S L A D E S L N P R
R A O B M U M L N P E
E E C W A R P I H U V
A E K J I N X K O P O
K S E E M O R E J Y E
```

USE THE LEFTOVER LETTERS TO SPELL
OUT A SECRET MESSAGE.

OKAY, I THINK I FOUND THEM ALL...
SO, **NOW** WHAT?
NOW...
...**MORE PIE!**
STARFIRE! IT'S **ME!** SNAP OUT OF IT!
SHOO, FLY! DO NOT BOTHER ME!
SMACK
OH NO SHE **DIDN'T!**

STARFIRE, THERE'S ***ONE*** CHALLENGE LEFT AND IT'S ALL UP TO YOU. YOUR TEAM IS ***COUNTING*** ON ***YOU!***

BUT I AM ENJOYING THE PIE!

WHILE BEAST BOY RAN A RACE AND CYBORG USED HIS BRAIN FOR HIS CHALLENGE...

YOUR CHALLENGE IS...

STARFIRE

...A RACE AGAINST ***THE BRAIN!***

THE BRAIN

DUDE, THIS SHOULD BE A PIECE OF CAKE! THE BRAIN DOESN'T EVEN HAVE LEGS!
DO YOU NOT MEAN A "PIECE OF PIE"?
STARFIRE

THAT'S GOTTA BE SOME...UNGH... STRONG MOJO IN THOSE PIES!
SO, LET'S BEGIN OUR "RACE" TO ANSWER THE MOST QUESTIONS CORRECTLY BEFORE TIME RUNS OUT!

WHO IS THE FOUNDER OF THE HIVE ACADEMY?
UM, THAT WOULD BE--
BZZT
TIME'S UP!

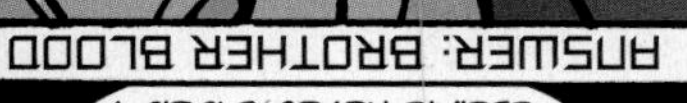
ANSWER: BROTHER BLOOD

ACCORDING TO THE NURSERY RHYME, "FOUR AND TWENTY BLACKBIRDS" ARE BAKED IN A WHAT?
PIE.
DING
CORRECT!

WHO COMES FROM DIMENSION 4 AND 9/8THS?
OH, THAT IS--
BZZT
TIME'S UP!
ANSWER: LARRY THE TITAN

A CIRCLE GRAPH DIVIDED INTO PIECES IS ALSO KNOWN AS WHAT TYPE OF CHART?
PIE.
DING

WHAT IS THE NAME OF JOHNNY RANCID'S DOG?
I BELIEVE IT WAS--
BZZT

ANSWER: WREX

SHEPHERDS, ESKIMOS AND MUD ALL HAVE WHAT IN COMMON?
PIE.
DING

NAME THE EPISODE THAT INTRODUCED AQUALAD.
"EPISODE"...?
BZZT
ANSWER: DEEP SIX

THE NUMBER "3.14159265" IS ALSO KNOWN AS...
PI.
DING

DING DING DING
AND THAT SIGNALS THE END OF OUR TRIVIA ROUND AND THE END OF OUR GAME!

LOOKING AT OUR SCOREBOARD, IT'S TITANS WITH ZERO POINTS...AND PIE WITH 9,997 POINTS!
SCOREBOARD
TITANS 0
PIE 9,997
ROBIN SAID TO WAIT, BUT I CAN TAKE THIS GUY!

WE WERE UP AGAINST *PIE* THIS WHOLE TIME?!
WE NEVER STOOD A CHANCE!

HEY, CHARLIE! TELL THEM WHAT THEY *WOULD'VE* WON IF THEY WEREN'T SUCH *LOSERS!*
WHY, IT'S...
...A LIFETIMES MEMBERSHIP TO THE PIE OF THE HOUR CLUB!!!
LIFETIME MEMBER
PIE OF HOUR THE MONTH CLUB!
-SNIFF- SO NEAR -SNIFF- -SNIFF- BUT YET SO FAR...
OHHHH...
NOT TO WORRY, CHILDREN! WE DO HAVE SOME LOVELY *PARTING GIFTS* FOR YOU...
EAT! EAT!
THESE PEOPLE HAVE LOST THEIR *MINDS! I* CAN'T WAIT FOR ROBIN AND RAVEN ANY LONGER!
WHO WANT PIE?

PARDON ME, GOOD SIR!
BUT THERE SEEMS TO BE A FLY IN MY SOUP...

UH, FIRST OF ALL, THAT'S NOT SOUP!
AND SECONDLY, THAT'S NOT A FLY!

SHUT YOUR PIE HOLES ALREADY! STOP EATING THIS STUFF!

THAT TALKING BUG IS TRYING TO STEAL MY PIE!
WHO YOU CALLING A BUG?!
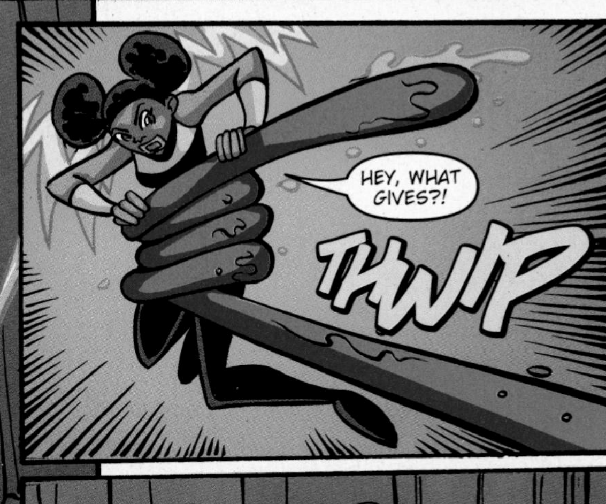
HEY, WHAT GIVES?!
THWIP

WHAT'S RAVEN'S FAVORITE PIE?
APPLE GRUMBLE!

GRR...

!!!
DIRTY NASTY GROSS ME OUT!!!
NOT TO WORRY, LITTLE FLY GIRL...PIE IS GOOD FOR WHATEVER AILS YOU!
STARFIRE... PUT DOWN THAT PIE!
AZARATH, METRION, ZINTHOS!
BONK
OW!
SMAK
OH!
SHAKE
SHAKE
SHAKE
WH-WHOA! WHOA! I'M G-GONNA BE S-S-SICK!

PLEASE, CHILDREN! MOTHER MAE-EYE ONLY WANTED TO--

WHAT? BRAINWASH US AGAIN? TAKE OVER OUR LIVES? MAKE US YOUR SLAVES?

ACTUALLY...I WAS JUST TRYING TO SELL A ***GAME SHOW*** TO THE TV NETWORKS!

MOTHER TRIED TO GET HER OWN ***COOKING*** SHOW, BUT THEY TOLD ME I WASN'T ***YOUNG*** AND ***HIP*** ENOUGH!

SO, I TRIED TO COME UP WITH A DIFFERENT KIND OF PROGRAM, SOMETHING ***WILD*** AND ***FUN!***

AND YOU LURED US HERE BECAUSE...?

I NEEDED STAR POWER!
PEOPLE LOVE THE TEEN TITANS ALMOST AS MUCH AS MOTHER DOES...
PIE WILL BE MY UNDOING!
OH, ROBIN, THE MOTHER MAE-EYE DID NOT DO ANY REAL HARM AND SHE WAS CLEARLY ATTEMPTING THE CHANGE OF CAREER, SO MAY WE NOT JUST...LET HER GO?
I DON'T KNOW ABOUT THAT, STARFIRE...
...MAYBE IF SHE PROMISES TO STOP BAKING HER PURPLE POISON PIES...

I SAY NO MORE PIES OF ANY KIND!

YOU M-MEAN... NOT EVEN... APPLE PIES?

NO.

...PUMPKIN PIE?

NO.

WHAT ABOUT PECAN PIE?

PECAN? WELL...

NO! NO CHERRY, BLUEBERRY, BLACKBERRY, RHUBARB, SWEET POTATO, KEY LIME, SUGAR, CHOCOLATE, COCONUT CREAM, BANANA CREAM, ANY KIND OF CREAM OR ANY OTHER KIND OF PIE!

NOT EVEN...PIZZA PIE?
!
END

THIS THING'S *UNSTOPPABLE!*
AND I'M RUNNING OUT OF *ARROWS!*
SLINGS & ARROWS

WHERE WOULD YOU BE WITHOUT THOSE ARROWS?
THE SAME PLACE YOU'D BE WITHOUT WATER, FISH BOY!

ALL RIGHT, POP QUIZ. SUPER VILLAIN DRIVING A GIANT SQUID. SQUIDDY'S TOO BIG TO TAKE DOWN. WHAT DO YOU DO?

SHOOT THE DRIVER!

SHHWIP
PAFF
!
PLOOSH
RRRRRAAAH!
OKAY, THAT DIDN'T WORK! I'M GOING AFTER TRIDENT! WE CAN'T LET HIM ESCAPE!
OH, SURE! LEAVE ME WITH THE BIG ONE!

WHY DO YOU WASTE YOUR TIME WITH THE SURFACE DWELLERS, AQUALAD?!

JOIN ME AND HELP ME TAKE OVER THE WORLD ABOVE!

AND IF I SAY NO? YOU GONNA USE MIND CONTROL LIKE YOU DID ON THE SQUID MONSTER?

HAVE IT YOUR WAY, LAND LOVER!

KRZZT
UNGH!

!

DON'T WORRY, BUDDY...

SHHWIP

BLOOP

...I'VE GOT YA COVERED!

YOU KNOW, TRIDENT..THERE'S NOTHING UNGH WRONG WITH USING YOUR BRAIN...

...BUT YOU SHOULD RE-THINK THE MIND CONTROL THING...

WHO...?

GLURGGGGGG!
BZZZT
BZZZT

...AND JUST TRY ASKING NICELY!
TRUST ME! IT WORKS! RIGHT, GUYS?

WHOA!
HEY! EASY THERE, GRABBY GUS!

ONE TRICK ARROW LEFT...

...AND IT HAPPENS TO BE SOMETHING MY BUDDY CYBORG JUST SENT ME...

...AND NOW'S AS GOOD A TIME AS ANY TO GET LOUD...

BOOM

SEE YA! WOULDN'T WANNA BE YA!
KROOOOOSH
SPEEDY! I COULD USE A HAND OVER HERE!
A HAND? AND WHERE WERE YOU WHEN I HAD EIGHT OF THEM GRABBING AT ME TO PLAY "MARCO POLO"?
WHAT? YOU THINK TRIDENT JUST DECIDED TO TAKE A NAP OVER HERE?
HA! A NAP! YOU'RE PRETTY FUNNY FOR SOMEONE WHO SMELLS LIKE A SEAWEED SANDWICH RIGHT NOW!
AND YOU'RE A LAUGH RIOT FOR SOMEONE WHOSE BREATH ALWAYS SMELLS LIKE THEY JUST ATE A SEAWEED SANDWICH!

WELL, THAT COULD'VE BEEN A LOT WORSE!
EASY FOR **YOU** TO SAY! YOU'VE STILL GOT A WHOLE **OCEAN** OF WATER...
...BUT **I'M** ALL OUT OF ARROWS!

I WISH THERE WAS A WAY TO GO DOWN THERE AND RETRIEVE SOME OF MY ARROWS... *HINT-HINT!*
DON'T WORRY, I'M SURE TRAMM CAN HOOK YOU UP WITH SOME NEW GEAR. AND MAYBE YOU CAN ASK CYBORG TO SEND YOU MORE "SONIC ARROWS."

BUT, YOU MIGHT WANNA BRUSH UP YOUR BODIES OF WATER. THAT'S ACTUALLY...A...**LAKE**... BACK...THERE?
KRRSSSH

AND LOOK WHAT **ELSE** IS BACK THERE!

WAIT!
IT'S... IT'S TRYING TO COMMUNICATE...

WHAT'S IT SAYING?

IT'S... APOLOGIZING...
IT SAYS SORRY, BUT TRIDENT MADE IT ATTACK US!

YEAH, AND HOW MANY TIMES HAVE WE HEARD *THAT* FROM A SUPER VILLAIN LACKEY!
BUT HOW MANY TIMES HAVE ANY OF THEM...
...EVER RETURNED YOUR ARROWS?
YOU KNOW, I SHOULDA LEARNED FROM THAT TIME I FOUGHT PLASMUS WITH ROBIN AND THE OTHERS...
...SOMETIMES I DON'T WANT THE ARROWS BACK!

END

I NEED A BETTER POWER SOURCE FOR MY LIGHT SUIT, PROFESSOR CHANG! NONE OF THE ONES YOU SOLD ME ARE SUFFICIENT FOR MY NEEDS!
I REGRET THAT I CAN BE OF NO FURTHER ASSISTANCE TO YOU, DR. LIGHT. I GAVE YOU THE BEST POWER CELLS AND BATTERIES THAT MONEY CAN BUY. I SUGGEST YOU TRY ANOTHER "SUPPLIER"...
THE BATTERY

SO, WHEN WILL HE GET THIS PACKAGE?
SpdEx
Ground
IT'S GUARANTEED TO BE IN STEEL CITY AND DELIVERED TO TITANS EAST TOWER BEFORE NOON TOMORROW!
RIGHT ON! SPEEDY DELIVERY FOR SPEEDY THE TITAN! THANKS!
SPEAKING OF SPEED...I'LL RACE YA TO "PIZZA SHACK"!
LAST ONE THERE PAYS!
FALSE START! NO FAIR!
YO! CHEATERS NEVER PROSPER!

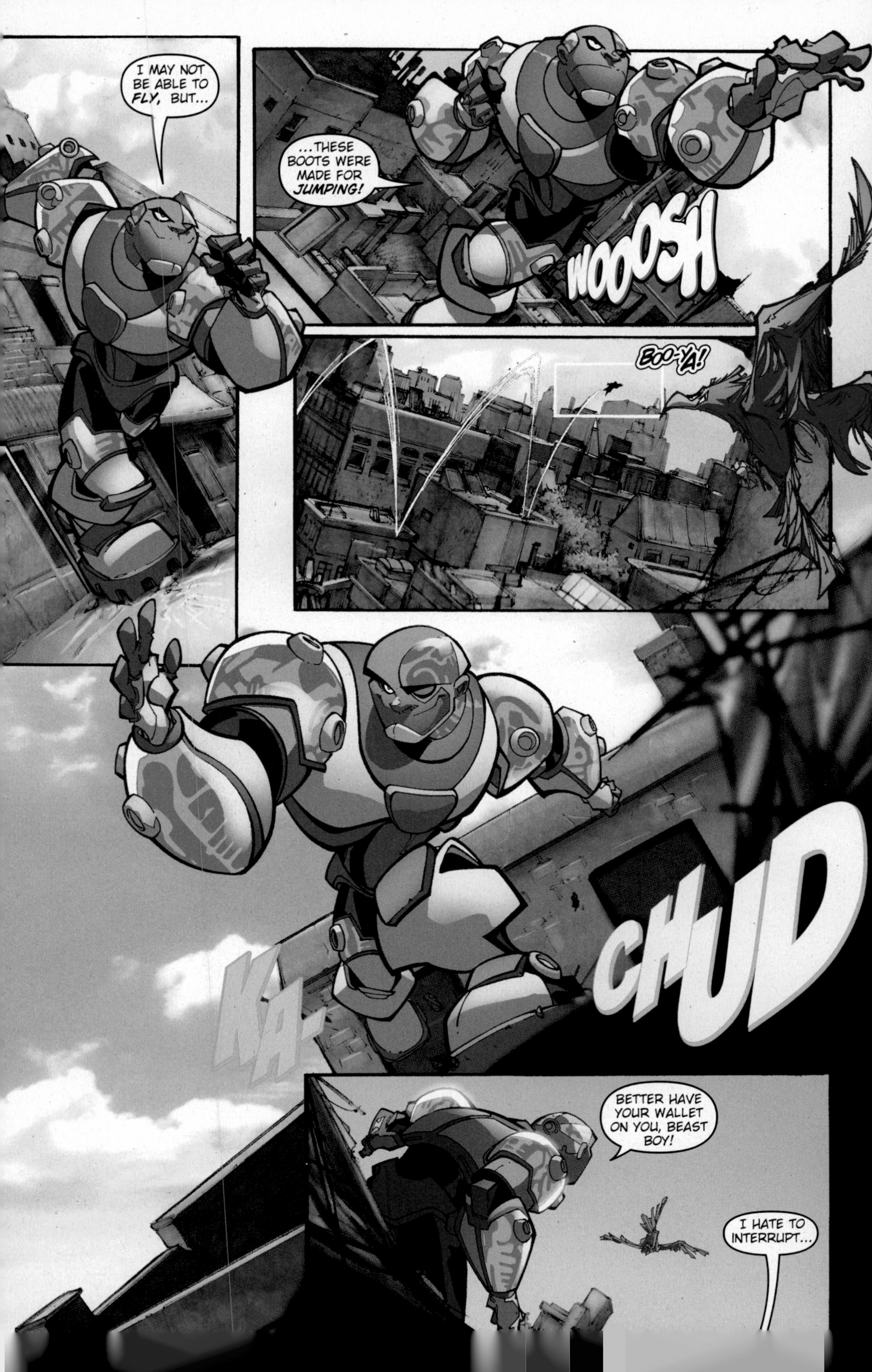
I MAY NOT BE ABLE TO FLY, BUT...
...THESE BOOTS WERE MADE FOR JUMPING!
WOOOSH
BOO-YA!
KA-CHUD
BETTER HAVE YOUR WALLET ON YOU, BEAST BOY!
I HATE TO INTERRUPT...

...BUT I'M GOING TO ANYWAY.
DR. LIGHT!
I'M GLAD TO SEE YOU REMEMBER ME, CYBORG.
YEAH, I REMEMBER YOU ALL RIGHT! I REMEMBER THE TITANS KICKING YOUR BUTT ON MORE THAN ONE OCCASION!
CH-CHUK CH-CHUK
WHRAM
THAT WAS THEN, THIS IS NOW!
WHOMP
RAAAWK

I WONDER WHAT ROAST BALD EAGLE TASTES LIKE!
WHRAM
DON'T KNOW ABOUT THAT, BUT HOW ABOUT A TASTE OF KNUCKLE SANDWICH!
WHAM
BASH
NAH.
I'M TRYING TO CUT DOWN ON CRABS.

WAP WAP WAP
COME OUTTA THERE, YOU COWARD!
OR LET ME IN SO I CAN TEACH YOU NOT TO PICK A FIGHT WITH THE TITANS!
LET YOU IN? OKAY...
B.B.!
FFFWASH
AAAAAH!

DO I HAVE YOUR UNDIVIDED ATTENTION, CYBORG?
OR DO I HAVE TO CAUSE YOUR LITTLE GREEN FRIEND HERE EVEN MORE PAIN?
M-MY EYES...I C-CAN'T SEE...
DON'T YOU DARE--
FINE! WHAT DO YOU WANT!?
LET'S MAKE THIS QUICK THEN...
GIVE ME YOUR POWER CELL.
MY WHAT?!
YOUR BATTERY. I WANT IT. NOW.
I'M UPGRADING MY LIGHT SUIT, AND WORD ON THE STREET IS YOU'VE GOT THE JUICE I NEED.
THEN YOU CAN COME OUT HERE AND GET IT, BUT I HOPE YOU LIKE LOTS OF PULP!
YOU DON'T SCARE ME, YOU OVERSIZED WIND-UP TOY.
THEN DROP YOUR FORCE FIELD AND HELP YOURSELF TO MY POWER CELL, DOC.
OH, I WILL. AS SOON AS YOU DROP YOUR WEAPONS.

I WON'T LET YOU GET AWAY WITH THIS...
KLIK CHIK KLIK CHIK
ALL OF YOUR WEAPONS.
CH-CHIK
KLANG
I SAID, ALL OF YOUR WEAPONS.
CH-CHIK CH-CHIK
POIT POIT POIT POIT
TAKE IT AS A COMPLIMENT, CYBORG... I'M NOT SETTLING FOR LESS THAN THE UNMATCHED CAPACITY AND LONG LIFE OF YOUR BATTERY TO POWER MY WONDEROUS LIGHT SUIT...YOU SHOULD BE HONORED.

WHAT IS ALL OF THIS?!
I'M A SUPER VILLAIN, NOT A MECHANIC! WHICH ONE IS THE BATTERY?! HURRY UP! I'VE WASTED ENOUGH TIME HERE!
IT'S RIGHT THERE, UNDER THE HYPERSONIC CONDUCTORS, BESIDE THE ELECTROSURGE CONTROLLER.
UNDER THE HYPER WHICH AND BESIDE THE ELECTRO WHAT?
FOR A DUDE CALLED DR. LIGHT, YOU'RE NOT SO BRIGHT, ARE YA?
IT'S THE BLUE CYLINDRICAL OBJECT, YOU DUMMY! THE BLUE THINGIE! JUST GRAB IT ALREADY...
AH! THE BLUE THINGIE! WHY DIDN'T YOU JUST SAY...

KRRZZZT
KRRZZT
...SOOOOOOH!
HAW-HAW! NOT VERY BRIGHT AT ALL!
WELL, HE WANTED MORE POWER SO I GAVE IT TO HIM.
BE CAREFUL WHAT YOU WISH FOR, HUH?
I... HATE... YOU...
END

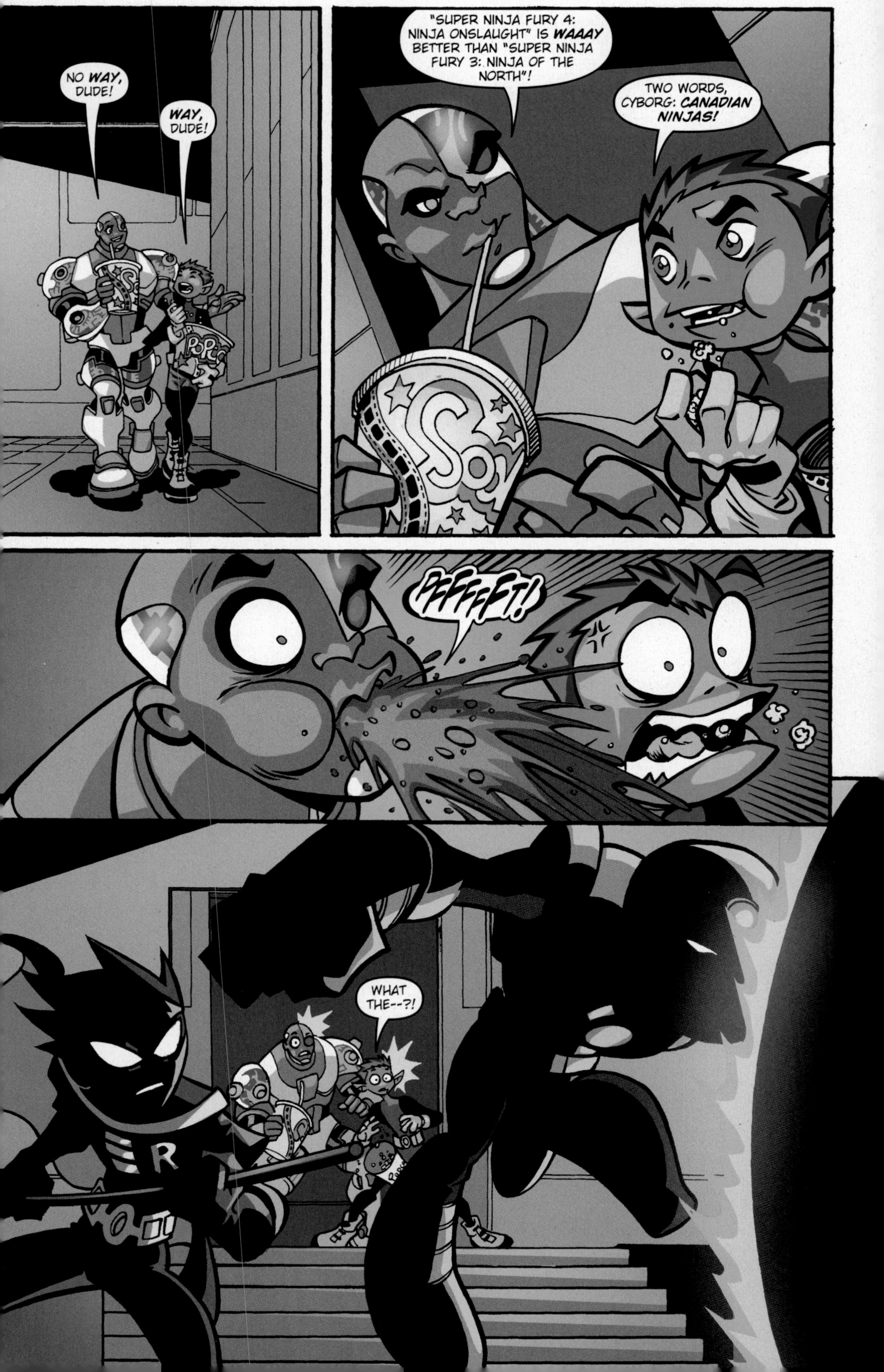

PFFFFFT!

WHAT THE--?!

THIS ISN'T OVER!

ROBIN!
DUDE! WHAT ISN'T OVER...???

AND WHO **WAS** THAT?
DON'T WORRY ABOUT IT. IT'S BEEN TAKEN CARE OF.
THAT'S IT? THAT'S ALL WE GET? "IT'S BEEN TAKEN CARE OF"?

BUT WHAT ABOUT THE DUDE WHO WAS JUST HERE? I DIDN'T LIKE THE LOOK OF HIM!--HE LOOKED LIKE... WARP: THE JUNIOR HIGH YEARS!
HEY! WHERE ARE YOU GOING?
TO THE RACE TRACK TO BET ON SOME PONIES.

SAY WHAT? WE JUST HAD A HOME INVASION AND YOU'RE--
WAIT A MINUTE--! SINCE WHEN DID YOU BECOME A **GAMBLER?**

IT'S NOT GAMBLING WHEN YOU KNOW WHO'S GOING TO WIN!
HE'S BEEN ACTING **REALLY** WEIRD SINCE HE GOT BACK EARLY FROM TRAINING WITH BUSHIDO...

A WEEK LATER...
NO WAY, DUDE!
WAY!
I CHANGED MY MIND! "SNF3" IS THE BETTER MOVIE!
WRONG! NOW THAT I'VE SEEN "SNF4" FIVE TIMES I'M "NINJA ONSLAUGHT" ALL THE WAY!
PFFFT!
YOU GETTIN' THAT FEELING OF DÉJÀ-VU...?

RAVEN, IT'S ME!
NIGHT TIME

ANOTHER INTRUDER!
BUT I JUST UPGRADED THE TOWER'S SECURITY SYSTEM! NO ONE SHOULD BE ABLE TO GET PAST IT!
NO ONE... EXCEPT YOU!
YOU WERE SO PROUD OF THE SECURITY SYSTEM... ALMOST AS PROUD AS WHEN YOU FIGURED OUT HOW TO SEND ME BACK HERE. IF ONLY YOU WERE SURE OF HOW TO GET ME HO--
I DON'T KNOW WHAT YOU'RE TALKING ABOUT, MISTER, BUT MAKE ANOTHER MOVE AND--
Gasp! FRIENDS! NO!
WHAT TIME IS IT WHEN A CROCODILE EATS YOUR ALARM CLOCK?

DO NOT HARM HIM!
HELLO, PRINCESS.
YOU *KNOW* THIS CREEP, STARFIRE?
WAIT A MINUTE...

...ROBIN?

ACTUALLY, IT'S *NIGHTWING* NOW.
HOW DOES THE EXPRESSION GO? "LONG... TIME...NO SEE"?

SO, THE DUDE FROM LAST WEEK ***WAS*** WARP, THE TIME-TRAVELING THIEF?

AND HE CAME FROM THE SAME PLACE YOU DID... IN THE ***FUTURE?***

YES, THAT WAS WARP, BUT A ***YOUNGER*** VERSION AND NOT THE ONE YOU KNOW. AND YES, HE CAME FROM THE FUTURE LIKE ME... WHERE HE'S A ***TITAN.***

OKAY, ***THAT'S*** THE PART TRIPPIN' ME UP! WARP WAS, I MEAN, ***IS,*** I MEAN ***IS GOING TO BE*** A TEEN TITAN IN THE FUTURE?!

ACTUALLY, FOR A WHILE THERE HE WAS THE ONLY ***TEEN*** TITAN. WE STOPPED CALLING OURSELVES THE "TEEN" TITANS BECAUSE THE REST OF US WERE...

OLDER.

YOU WILL ALL RECALL THAT I ONCE TRAVELED FORWARD IN THE TIME AND SAW THE US OF THE FUTURE.

THERE, WE DESTROYED THE DEVICE WHICH ALLOWED THE WARP TO TRAVEL THROUGH THE TIME AND IT TURNED BACK HIS BIOLOGICAL CLOCK AND HE REVERTED INTO AN INFANT...

SEE EPISODE: HOW LONG IS TOMORROW

YES, YOU LEFT "BABY WARP" IN OUR CARE. HE GREW UP. WE TRAINED HIM. HE BECAME A TITAN.
WHAT TIME IS IT WHEN A CROCODILE EATS YOUR ALARM CLOCK?
FOR HIM, IT'S LUNCH TIME!

BUT NO MATTER WHAT WE DID, HE COULDN'T RESIST HIS FASCINATION WITH TIME TRAVEL. BY AGE TEN, HE REBUILT HIS OWN TECH.
HE FOUGHT ALONGSIDE THE TITANS FOR A TIME. HE WAS GOOD. HE BATTLED EVIL, BUT...
...AS WE'VE SEEN BEFORE, EVEN TEEN TITANS CAN BE TEMPTED DOWN THE WRONG PATH...
SO, WARP FULFILLED HIS ULTIMATE DESTINY AND BECAME A BAD GUY AGAIN...IT DIDN'T MATTER WHO HE WAS WITH OR WHERE IN TIME--
DON'T WORRY, RAVEN. IF YOU'RE WORRIED ABOUT YOUR--
HOLD UP! I DON'T THINK WE SHOULD BE GETTING INTO THIS. WE'VE HEARD MORE THAN ENOUGH ALREADY. IT'S NOT RIGHT TO KNOW THE FUTURE...
UNLESS IT CAN HELP CHANGE THE PAST AND STOP SOMEONE LIKE THE WARP.
WHICH BRINGS ME TO WHY I'M HERE.

R-ROBIN...? WHAT ARE YOU DOING HERE?
IS SOMETHING WRONG?

ON THE CONTRARY, EVERYTHING SEEMS TO BE GOING JUST RIGHT.

AND WHO ARE YOU?
YOU KNOW THE MYSTERIOUS INVESTOR WHO THIS MORNING BOUGHT OUT EVERYONE ELSE AND NOW OWNS 100% OF THIS DEVELOPMENT?

YOU'RE LOOKING AT HIM!

EXIT
CAN YOU SOLVE THESE PICTURE PUZZLES?

WHY WOULD THE TEENAGED WARP FROM THE FUTURE WANT TO KILL TEENAGED ROBIN IN THE PAST???

OH-NO! DOES GROWN-UP ROBIN BECOME SOME KIND OF EVIL DESPOT IN THE YEAR 2020? AND WE, LIKE, HAVE TO KILL HIM BEFORE HE CONQUERS THE WORLD AND MAKES EVERYONE DRESS IN CHRISTMAS COLORS ALL THE TIME?!?!
UH, NO... YOU'RE LOOKING AT "GROWN-UP ROBIN."

OH, RIGHT.
THE OLDER WARP TRAVELED FROM THE FUTURE BEYOND MY TIME AND WENT BACK TO THE PAST BEYOND NOW...

...TO A PARTICULARLY VULNERABLE TIME IN MY YOUTH AND...CHANGED THE COURSE OF HISTORY BY BECOMING MY MENTOR...

THAT'S WHY ROBIN'S BEEN ACTING STRANGE LATELY, LIKE HE'S NOT HIMSELF.
AND THAT EXPLAINS HIS RECENT INTEREST IN THE STOCK MARKET!
AND GAMBLING!
www.STocks.com
RACE
RACE
HORSES

NEW TOW
REAL ESTATE LISTINGS
AND THE REAL ESTATE!

WELL DONE, MY "SON." ALL THE MONEY YOU'VE MADE IS HELPING BUILD MY FUTURE EMPIRE!
IT'S EASY TO PICK THE WINNING HORSE OR THE STOCK THAT WILL GO UP IN VALUE WHEN YOU'VE GOT SOMEONE FROM THE FUTURE "ADVISING" YOU.
OF COURSE, WE COULD HAVE JUST STOLEN THE MONEY OR TAKEN THINGS BY FORCE, BUT THIS WAY WE DO IT ON THE SLY BEHIND THE TITANS' BACKS.
THEY WON'T KNOW WHAT *HIT* THEM! JUST LIKE THEY WON'T SEE YOU COMING WHEN THE TIME COMES FOR YOU TO TAKE THEM DOWN.
WHICH WILL BE **SOON,** RIGHT?
"SOON"?

WHY WAIT?
THERE'S NO TIME LIKE THE PRESENT.
AND PRESENTLY IT IS...
...GO TIME!
STARFIRE, I'M COUNTING ON YOU! YOU'RE GOING TO TURN THIS TIDE...
ME? I DO NOT WANT TO HURT YOU, I MEAN, ROBIN... I MEAN, HOW AM I TO...?
DON'T WORRY, YOU'LL KNOW WHEN THE TIME COMES!
NO! NOT YET! THIS ISN'T HOW IT'S SUPPOSED TO HAPPEN! YOU'RE NOT SUPPOSED TO BE HERE!
FUNNY, I WAS ABOUT TO SAY THE SAME THING TO YOU!
EXIT
CAN YOU SOLVE THESE PICTURE PUZZLES?
TIME OUT!
TIME FLIES!
I NEED MORE TIME TO FIGURE IT OUT...

FWWIP
AZARATH... METRION...
GOOD THING I LEARNED SOME NEW MOVES FROM "SNF4"!
I HEAR "SUPER NINJA FURY 9" WILL BE THE BEST OF THE SERIES!

SHHHRAK
HUP!
SMAK
Mmmf!
Rrruh!
???
SLIP

HOW DID YOU DISCOVER MY PLAN?!
SHHRING
SHHHRING
A LITTLE BIRDY FROM THE FUTURE TOLD ME!
SHHRING
SHHHRING
WHAT?! I WAS BETRAYED!!!
BY SOMEONE WHO COULD RESIST THE GOOD IN HIM ABOUT AS WELL AS YOU RESISTED THE BAD IN YOU...
YOU SHOULD'VE KNOWN ME BETTER THAN THAT, WARP!
KNOCK-KNOCK.
WHO IS THERE?
JUSTIN!
JUSTIN WHO?
JUSTIN TIME TO HELP ME STOP WARP!

GET OFF MY BACK!
NOT UNTIL I DISCONNECT YOUR POWER CELL!
STARFIRE! TAKE HIM DOWN! HE KNOWS OUR WEAKNESSES!
AND I... I THINK I KNOW HIS...
ROBIN! LISTEN TO ME!
YOU MUST STOP THIS! YOU MUST STOP THIS BECAUSE...
!!!

YOU'RE WASTING MY TIME!

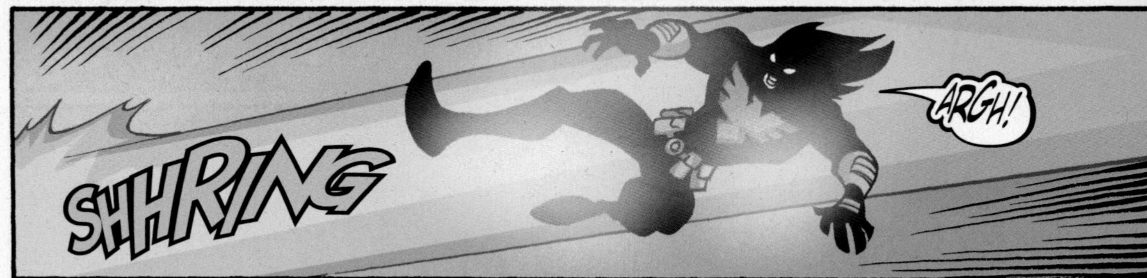
SHHRING
ARGH!

NIGHTWING!
STAR... STARFIRE...?

COME ALONG, BOY! WE MUST--
WH-WHAT'S HAPPENING TO ME...?

TOO LATE! RUNNING OUT OF TIME! HISTORY REPEATING!

I SHOULD... GO...BEFORE THAT PORTAL CLOSES...
LET CYBORG OFF THE HOOK... HITCH A RIDE HOME...
WAIT! WHAT ABOUT ROBIN! WHERE HAS HE GONE?!
HE HASN'T GONE ANYWHERE... THE WRINKLES IN TIME CAUSED BY WARP SHOULD IRON THEMSELVES OUT NOW THAT WE'VE FOILED HIS PLANS...
YOU TOLD...ROBIN... WHAT HE NEEDED TO HEAR... SOON, HE'LL BE BACK WHERE HE BELONGS...
NOW I SHOULD GO BACK TO WHERE I BELONG...
ARE YOU CERTAIN ABOUT ROBIN...?
DON'T WORRY! HE'LL BE ALL RIGHT!
JUST LOOK AT ME!

WHY AREN'T YOU EATING, BEAST BOY?

THINKING ABOUT THIS TIME TRAVEL STUFF MADE ME LOSE MY APPETITE...I MEAN, HOW COULD GOOD GROWN-UP ROBIN OF TOMORROW BE IN THE SAME PLACE AS EVIL ROBIN TODAY IN THE PRESENT?
AND HOW IS IT POSSIBLE FOR WARP TO TRAVEL FORWARD IN TIME TO BECOME YOUNGER AND GO TO THE PAST WHERE HE'S OLDER? AND HOW'S IT ALL GONNA AFFECT THE FUTU--
IT'S CALLED "TIME TRAVEL PARADOX." WE CAN'T MAKE SENSE OF IT BECAUSE WE DON'T FULLY UNDERSTAND TIME TRAVEL YET.
WE DON'T EVEN KNOW HOW WHAT'S HAPPENED WILL AFFECT THE FUTURE, IF AT ALL. SO, IT'S POINTLESS TO WORRY ABOUT IT NOW.
CITY PIZZA
TY PIZZA
PIZ

AWESOME! YOU ORDERED PIZZA! I'M STARVING!

Grrr...
IT'S OKAY, BEAST BOY! I THINK IT'S REALLY HIM, BACK HOME ON TIME JUST LIKE HE'S SUPPOSED TO BE...
OH, ROBIN, YOU ARE SEEMINGLY UNHARMED!

OF COURSE I AM! WHY WOULDN'T I BE? I WAS ONLY TRAINING WITH BUSHIDO FOR A COUPLE OF WEEKS...
WHAT'S GOING ON HERE?
SNIFF-SNIFF
IT IS A LOOOONG STORY.

Um, OKAY! TELL ME ALL ABOUT IT! I'VE GOT ALL THE TIME IN THE WORLD...
END

JUMP CITY.
BEAST BOY! OH, BEEEEEAST BOY!
WHERE ARE YOU, BEAST BOY?

SORRY, DON'T REMEMBER SEEING HIM AROUND HERE.
MIGHT YOU BE IN THERE?
LOST
Pet's Wo
PUPPIES

PLEASE, SIR. PERHAPS YOU HAVE SEEN OUR FRIEND?
HMM...I DON'T THINK SO.
LOST

BEAST BOY! WHERE ARE YOU, BEAST BOY!
ANSWERS TO BEAST BOY
HAVE YOU SEEN THIS AARDVARK?

PRIVATE HIVE! PRIVATE HIVE!
PRIVATE HIVE! PRIVATE HIVE!
PRIVATE HIVE!
WINNER AND STILL CHAMPEEN...
PRIVATE HIVE!
ARENA

SOME COME HERE FOR THE SPECTACLE. OTHERS TO MAKE WAGERS. THEN THERE ARE THOSE WITH DIFFERENT AGENDAS...
ATLAS CAME TO TRAIN AND COMPETE. THE MASTER OF GAMES RECRUITED FOR HIS OWN TOURNAMENTS. EVEN SLADE CAME LOOKING FOR AN... "APPRENTICE" ONCE.
AND YOU, GENERAL IMMORTUS? WHY HAVE YOU COME TO THE ARENA TODAY?
NOW I KNOW HOW A PIÑATA FEELS!
BUT YOU WON'T GET ANY SWEET TREATS OUT OF ME...
HUH?
YAAAAAA!

THUNK

YOU ONLY GET "THE CLAW"!

I'D WATCH MY SIX IF I WERE YOU!

MY... *SIX?*
THAT'S MILITARY TALK FOR...
...WATCH YOUR BACK!

!

KLONK
THAT WILL LEAVE A MARK FOR SURE.
IMPRESSIVE MANEUVER. YOUR LATEST RECRUIT HAS POTENTIAL.
PRIVATE HIVE!
PRIVATE HIVE!
PRIVATE HIVE!
PRIVATE HIVE!
PRIVATE HIVE!
WHAT *IS* THIS PLACE?
GNARRK, WHERE *ARE* YOU?
IF YOU SEE ANYTHING YOU LIKE, MAKE ME AN OFFER, GENERAL.
OF COURSE, THE *WINNERS* WILL COST YOU MORE THAN THE LOSERS.
PREPARE THE "CAVEMAN" FOR THE NEXT BATTLE...

THE PACIFIC OCEAN.
WHAT DO YOU MEAN SOMEONE TRIED TO KIDNAP YOU?!
RAGGABAG GALAGGA!
TRAMM SAYS THEY WERE WORKING FOR SOMEONE CALLED "THE LANISTA"...
TITANS TOWER.
...AND IT SOUNDS LIKE THEY WERE TRYING TO "RECRUIT" TRAMM FOR SOME KIND OF COMPETITION!
IN ANCIENT ROME, LANISTAS WERE SLAVE TRADERS WHO BOUGHT AND SOLD FIGHTERS FOR GLADIATOR GAMES.
I WONDER IF THEY GOT TO PANTHA.
PANTHA?
I CALLED ALL TITANS TO SEE IF ANYONE'S HEARD FRO BEAST BOY. PANTHA IS ONE OF THREE NO ANSWERING BACK. AN I CAN'T TRACK ANY O THEIR T-COMMUNICATO SIGNALS EITHER.
ONE OF THREE?
THE ARENA.
"YEAH, NO WORD FROM KOLE AND GNARRK EITHER..."

I FOLLOWED THE TRAIL HERE...BUT WHERE *IS* HE?
MAYBE I SHOULD'VE CALLED ROBIN AND THE OTHERS FOR HELP!
SHUNK
GUH...GUH... GNARRK...?
GNARRK!
I'LL TAKE THAT BET! A HUNDRED ON HIVE!
FIVE TO ONE ON THE NEANDERTHAL!

GNARRK
GNARRK...?
KACHAK
KACHAK
HA. THIS WON'T BE MUCH OF A MATCH. THE MOB WILL WANT THEIR MONEY BACK.
THIS WON'T DO!
MAKE THAT CRO-MAGNON FIGHT!
NO!
LEAVE HIM ALONE!

WHAP
EEEEE!
ZZZAAP
GNAAARR!
INCOMING!
KLANK
WHAT PART OF THE BODY IS LIKE A MUSICAL INSTRUMENT?

KRRANG...?
DEEEE-RECT HIT!
OOF!
SNEAK ATTACK!
THAT LITTLE ONE WITH THE PINK HAIR WASN'T PART OF THE PROGRAM... BUT THE MOB IS LOVING THIS!
WHY DID YOU BRING GNARRK HERE? WHY ARE YOU DOING THIS?
ISN'T IT OBVIOUS?

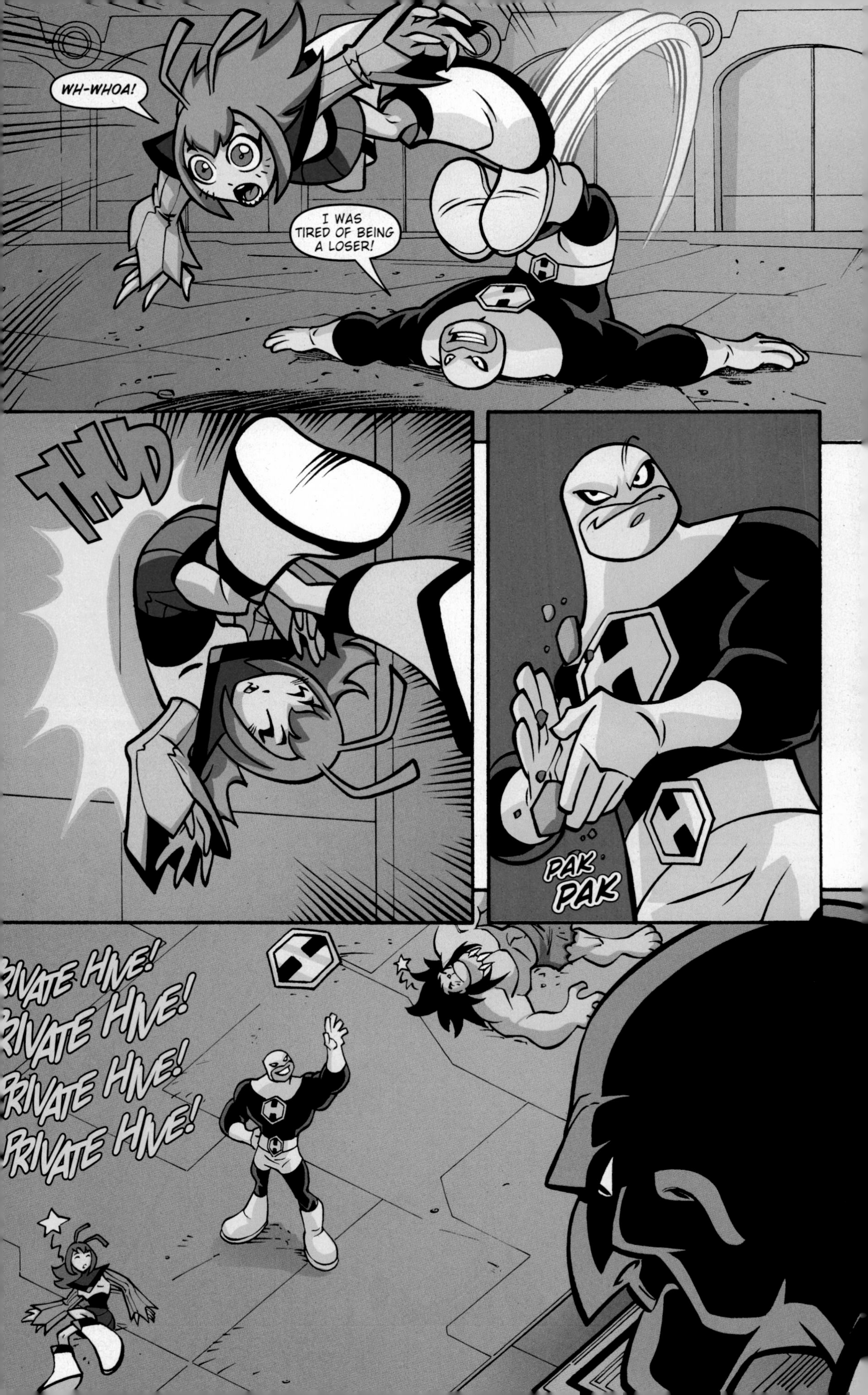
WH-WHOA!
I WAS TIRED OF BEING A LOSER!
THUD
PAK PAK
RIVATE HIVE!
RIVATE HIVE!
PRIVATE HIVE!
PRIVATE HIVE!

ELSEWHERE...
NO SIGN OF BEAST BOY.
BUT THIS IS LIKE LOOKING FOR A NEEDLE IN A HAYSTACK.
I HAVE GOOD NEWS AND BAD NEWS FOR YOU, HERALD.
THE BAD NEWS: PANTHA, KOLE, AND GNARRK ARE MISSING TOO.
ROBIN CAN'T SEEM TO REACH ANY OF THEM. SO, EITHER THE SIGNALS ARE BEING JAMMED OR SOMEONE'S MESSED WITH THEIR COMMUNICATORS OR... WORSE.
WHAT'S THE GOOD NEWS?
WE SUSPECT THEY MAY BE TOGETHER, HELD CAPTIVE BY THE SAME PERSON.
AND THIS IS GOOD NEWS BECAUSE?
WE MAY NOT BE ABLE TO TRACE THEIR COMMUNICATORS, BUT FOUR SUPER-POWERED ENERGY SIGNATURES IN ONE PLACE?
I'M AN EMPATH. I CAN SENSE PEOPLE. IF THEY'RE NEARBY. IF THEY'VE BEEN THERE.
YOUR GABRIEL HORN CAN OPEN PORTALS ALL OVER THE PLANET AND EVEN BETWEEN DIMENSIONS. YOU CAN GO ALMOST ANYWHERE.
I DIG WHERE YOU'RE COMING FROM. YOU WANT US TO COMBINE OUR POWERS TO FIND THE OTHERS...
ALL RIGHT, LET'S JAM!
AZARATH. METRION. ZINTHOS.
TOON-TOO ROOOO

BACK AT THE ARENA...
SECURE THE GIRL BELOW WITH THE OTHERS...THE MOB IS GETTING RESTLESS, WANTING TO SEE MORE ACTION...TIME TO BRING OUT THE "CHANGELING."
SHUNK
ARRK! ARRK ARRK!
IT'S OKAY, HE CAN TAKE CARE OF HIMSELF. HE'LL BE ALL RIGHT...I THINK.
GRRR...

LISTEN UP, HIVE! YOU'VE MESSED WITH NOT ONE, NOT TWO, NOT THREE, BUT *FOUR* TITANS-- AND WHEN YOU MESS WITH *ANY* OF US, YOU MESS WITH *ALL* OF US!
WELL, THINGS ARE ABOUT TO GET MESSIER...
THIS ENDS *NOW!*
KACHAK
KACHAK
RONWR!
BRING IT, GRUNT!
?

IMMORTUS, RUN!
RUH?
NO ONE GOES AWOL ON MY--
HISSSSS
--WATCH?
KNOCK, KNOCK.
WHO'S THERE?
SNAKESKIN.
SNAKESKIN WHO?
SNAKESKIN BITE, SO LOOK OUT!

DROP AND GIVE ME TWENTY!
WH-CHUNK
OHHH... THAT'S CRUELTY TO ANIMALS, DUDE...
I SAID, **DROP**, SOLDIER!
LOOK OVER THERE, LANISTA!
WH-WHAT IS IT...?
IT'S THE PROVERBIAL CAVALRY! AND THE PROVERBIAL END OF THE SHOW!

HOLD IT RIGHT THERE!
TOON TOO ROOOO
THE WHACK-BEAST-BOY-IN-THE-HEAD LINE FORMS BEHIND ME!
WHAT PART OF THE BODY IS LIKE A MUSICAL INSTRUMENT?
THE NOSE! BECAUSE YOU CAN PICK IT AND BLOW IT!

I'M NOT BEAT, BUT I KNOW WHEN IT'S TIME TO **RETREAT!**
SSSPOOOFFF
BEAST BOY! TALK TO ME!
I CAN'T BELIEVE I JUST SAID THAT.
PANTHA... KOLE...AND GNARRK... DOWN BELOW...
I HOPE YOU ENJOY THIS NEXT NUMBER I'M ABOUT TO DROP!
HEH-HEH. "DROP"! CAN YOU DIG IT?
I KNEW THAT YOU COULD!

WHERE IS THE PRIVATE HIVE?
WE LOST HIM...
...BUT I'M SURE HE LIVES TO FIGHT ANOTHER DAY!
DON'T THINK I CAN'T SEE YOU THERE, TOGA MAN!
YOU'RE NEXT ON MY LIST!

ARE YOU GUYS COOL?
GNARRK! GNARRK!
SAY... H-HAVE YOU E-EVER CONSIDERED A CAREER AS A F-FIGHTER?
I ALREADY HAVE A CAREER AS A FIGHTER, FOOL...
A CRIME FIGHTER!
The End!